Also by Mary Swan

The Deep and Other Stories

THE BOYS IN THE TREES

THE BOYS
IN THE TREES

A Novel

MARY SWAN

A Holt Paperback
HENRY HOLT AND COMPANY
NEW YORK

Holt Paperbacks
Henry Holt and Company, LLC
Publishers since 1866
175 Fifth Avenue
New York, New York 10010
www.henryholt.com

A Holt Paperback® and ® are registered trademarks
of Henry Holt and Company, LLC.

Portions of this novel were previously published. "Naomi" was published
in *The Malahat Review* and "Long Exposure" in the *Harvard Review*.

Distributed in Canada by H. B. Fenn and Company Ltd.

Library of Congress Cataloging-in-Publication Data

Swan, Mary, date.
  The boys in the trees : a novel / Mary Swan.—1st Holt paperbacks ed.
    p. cm.
  ISBN-13: 978-0-8050-8670-6
  ISBN-10: 0-8050-8670-6
  1. Life change events—Fiction. 2. Psychological fiction. I. Title.
PR9199.4.S93B69 2008
813'.6—dc22   2007018569

Henry Holt books are available for special promotions
and premiums. For details contact: Director, Special Markets.

First Edition 2008

Designed by Victoria Hartman

Printed in the United States of America

1 3 5 7 9 10 8 6 4 2

For my friend Linda, first and ideal reader

And there are some who have no memorial,
who have perished as though they had not lived;
they have become as though they had not been born,
and so have their children after them.

—ECCLESIASTICUS 44:9

BEFORE

AND THEN HE was running through the long grass, wiping at the blood that made it hard to see but not slowing, still running. The roaring fell away behind and he knew that meant his father would turn on one of the others, that his mother would step into the worst of it, but he didn't care; at that moment he didn't even care. Still running when he reached the edge of the wood, dodging the whips from the spindly first trees, leaping and tripping over fallen, rotting trunks, running and running toward the dark heart of it. Not even slowing, not thinking when he saw the low, curved branch, jumped and pulled with his thin arms, climbed like an animal, bare toes gripping, until he was up where everything swayed and whispered, green leaves all around.

He wiped at his face again and felt the way his eye was swelling shut, tried to quiet his gasping breath. He didn't know what had brought the sudden kick, the fist to the head, but it wasn't worth wondering about; there was rarely a reason that anyone would recognize. He would have to go back, he knew that, but knew too that if he waited long enough his father would have worn himself out with the thick leather strap, the leg of the broken chair. Would have collapsed onto the bed like one of those mossy, fallen trees, battered knuckles trailing over the side.

His shirt was so thin it was like nothing at all and the rough bark scratched at his back where he leaned. He was well below the top of the tree but he could still see the whole world, see the long waving grass that had closed behind his escape, the green furred higher fields, the tilting cottage with a needle-thin spire of smoke rising. He could see the rutted track, curving away to the village, another clump of trees and the slate roof and highest windows of Bray Manor. When he turned his head a little there was a smudge of dark blue that he thought might be the sea, days away, and beyond that he didn't know, only that it would have to be someplace better.

Somehow after that first time he could easily find his way to the same tree, as if it was drawing him in, pulling him toward it and up and into the center of the green world. He knew there were creatures, spirits in the trees, but he wasn't afraid. Knew that if they had marked him out there was nothing he could do but believe it was not to do harm. He stole away when he could, often leaving things undone, and the way he climbed became like a well-worn path, one foot here, both there, the gouges where his toes fit, the bole under his clenched fingers. Once, from his perch, he saw his mother stepping out of the dark cottage doorway; that's who it had to be, although he was too far away to make out more than the faded shape of her. A few chickens came skittering, as they did when they heard the swish of her black skirts, but maybe he imagined that; from where he was the chickens would have been no more than shivers in the air. There or not there, his mother's hands must have been empty and she raised them and clasped them behind her head, tilted it back, and wedged in the vee of branches he did the same. There was a rare ray of sunlight that he supposed was warming her face and he tried to imagine how that felt, but the sun didn't reach him in the green heart of the wood, no way he could put himself in her place.

After a moment, no more, his mother turned back inside, and he picked up the knife from the spot where he'd balanced it, went back to his work. The idea to carve his name had come from somewhere, maybe the look of certain gouges in the bark, and he had slipped his father's knife from the jacket pocket, holding his breath. The babies watched him with their old eyes, but even if they could speak, he didn't think they would. There should have been time; he knew the sun would be high before his father snorted himself awake. But the tree was ancient, the wood like rock, like iron, and the tip of the knife snapped off, fell sparkling down through the leaves. He knew that the beating for a broken knife would be worse than for one that was missing, so he hid it in a hole he scooped out at the base of the tree, climbed like a pirate sometimes, the worn handle clenched between his teeth. He soon gave up the idea of his whole name, and worked instead at the straight lines of his initials. The wood was like iron and it was taking so long, but that was all right. He was still just a slip of a boy, a clout on the ear could send him flying, and he knew that he would have to be bigger, stronger, before he could leave. Thought maybe the time it would take to scrape out the letters would be a good measure. In fact, he was sure of it; it was one of the things he knew, in the same way he knew that he was just waiting here, that it was never meant to be his life.

Sometimes he sang while he worked, his voice twig-thin like his mother's at night, when she whispered about the trees that leaned over the green river. His own tree was so old, the branch so thick, that no sap welled in the wounds he made, but he knew it was there, deep inside. Knew that as surely as he knew that one day he would have money and a steep-roofed house with high windows, a family of his own that he would cherish. He knew that he would find the life he was meant to have, somewhere far from this terrible place, that all would be well, that one day people would know his name.

NAOMI—1871

Those dwelling in our cities are being educated in sanitary matters and modern treatments are proving more efficacious. There are fair prospects that the prevalence of this disease will soon be limited.

—*British Journal of Public Health*, June 1870

SADIE WAS BORN with a mass of dark hair and a strong cry and we named her for my mother. Though I didn't remember my mother at all, I thought she would have been pleased. William called through the door, *Is it all right? Is it all right?* and Bessie said, *A beautiful girl, I'll bring her out to you.* I'd told her once how he was about blood. I had been so tired but suddenly I felt that I could do anything and I sat up, thinking I should be the one to bring our child to him. But Bessie bade me lie back; she had finished the washing and wrapped Sadie in a blanket I had ready, only a sprig of dark hair showing, and she said over her shoulder that she would bring me a nice cup of tea but I didn't even hear the door closing, I fell into the most beautiful sleep of my life.

There was such a change in William when he sat with Sadie on his knee. The two lines between his eyebrows disappeared and he looked more like the boy he must have been, long before

I knew him. He sang her songs I'd never heard before, that must have come from his people. Songs about cruel sisters and sailing ships, and boys in the tall trees. My friends thought I was mad, with his stern look, his serious mouth, but when William sang to Sadie, I knew that I was right to join my life to his.

Cyanide of Mercury	gr. 1/3
Tincture of Aconite	M xv
Honey	℥xiij - M

Willie came with a worried look; my fault, for I couldn't stop fretting all the time I was carrying him. They say you forget the pain but I remembered enough and the churchyard was full of women, their babies growing without them. And besides, I didn't see how I could ever love another child as much as I loved my Sadie. William had been moved from the brickyard to the office, adding up figures all day. He came home with a pain behind his eyes instead of an aching back, but the hours were just as long. We had moved into a place with three rooms so that took up most of the extra money, and when it was time for the birth I had to send clear across town for Bessie, but she came without complaint. Annie Ashe down the stair took Sadie so she wouldn't hear my cries, a good thing. Bessie had to do some turning which hurt me a great deal, but she said it was nothing she hadn't seen before. She sent a boy to tell William and when he finally opened the door, holding Sadie by the hand, his eyes were bright like that time he drank ale on our wedding night.

There are many applications so equally good that it makes little difference which we employ. Sulphurous acid and glycerine, with the addition of thymol, is effectual and pleasant.

William's back and legs were covered in scars; he said he would never beat our children and he never did, though Tom sorely tried him at times. He was born early and all in a rush, Tom was; I had barely time to get to my bed. It was a Sunday morning and the sun was high, and Sadie was on a chair by our window, calling out the shapes she could see in the clouds. William shouted for Annie and she came running, her hands covered with flour. She meant well but her floured hands were rough and when Bessie came later, puffing, with her bonnet askew, I started to weep and could not stop.

Tom was a hard baby, crying to be fed every hour, wailing and wailing for no reason at all. Bessie came one day; I heard her groaning on the stairs. *It's a terrible thing to be old,* she said. My hair was down and knotted, all of us still in our nightclothes though it was well past ten o'clock. Tom howling and Willie banging on the pot with a wooden spoon and Sadie on her chair by the window, humming with her hands over her ears. *Lord love you,* Bessie said, *we can't have this—where's the Godfrey's? William doesn't like it,* I said, and she snorted and said, *No law says you have to tell him.* I climbed on a chair and brought down the steeple-shaped bottle of cordial, the same bottle she had given me when Sadie was born. She got a spoonful into Tom's wide-open mouth and sent me to dress; by the time I had put the last pin in my hair he was sound asleep and a pot of tea was steaming on the table, Willie and Sadie sitting quiet as mice, sucking on bits of peppermint. *What can I ever do for you,* I said, but Bessie said, *No more than you have done.* Her own children were grown and gone to London; they wrote letters sometimes, that she brought for me to read to her. It never took long.

I gave Tom another good dose in the evening, and he slept all through the night. *Maybe he's grown out of it,* William said, and

I just smiled, and thought that he looked a little different to me, though I couldn't have said just why.

• • •

There was a great change in William after the children, and my little doubts disappeared. My father had brought him home one night, after a talk in the Hall. *This is Mr. Heath,* he said, and I noticed the shine on his boots, though they were far from new. I lived a quiet life then, keeping house for my father. I had friends still from the neighborhood, from the time I was at school, and sometimes we would meet and laugh and laugh. But mostly they talked about their young men, and I found it strange, the things they could go on about. How this one had the most adorable ears, how that one couldn't abide a radish. Sometimes we went with the young men to a concert or a show of some kind, but I often wished myself home by the fire with a book in my hands, half listening for the stumbling sounds of my father's footsteps.

But then my father dropped like a stone, dead, they said, before he hit the ground. Rain dripped from the trees the day we buried him, a few friends from the shipyard, a distant aunt, and William, who held my arm and took me out to supper. His shiny boots were splashed with mud, like the hem of my dress. *Now you are all alone,* he said, *like me.* It was the way he spoke of himself; he'd been making his own way since he was a boy of eleven or twelve, although he had parents somewhere, and brothers and sisters and cousins. The knives were dull and a piece of meat shot from his plate; he bent to the floor and when he sat up again his cheeks were flushed. *I think we should marry,* he said. *I think that would be best.*

Bathe the feet in water as hot as it can be borne, until they glow. This may be necessary hourly for 2 to 3 days. At the same time apply towels wrung out of ice water to the forehead and throat. Every particle of the false membrane should be charred and removed at each sitting.

What we would have done without Bessie those weeks after Sadie was born, I don't know. She was a good baby—I knew how good once Tom came, but she was a great mystery to me. I knew nothing of babies, had only seen them lying asleep in a cradle, or in someone's arms in a shop or on the street. And William was just as baffled; he said he remembered nothing from his early life, from the birth of brothers and sisters, nothing but the thick piece of leather hanging by the door.

· · ·

Sadie loved to draw. I saved all the paper wrappings when I went to the shop and she could sit for hours at our table, lost, with one hand splayed on her forehead, pushing her hair up. She liked to draw the rivers and fields William told her about and she liked to draw all of us, standing together. *What are those,* I said, pointing to some lines arching over us, and she said, *Those are the trees, and those are the boys in the trees.* She left her pictures on the table with William's knife and plate; they were all asleep nights he came home but on early Saturdays they'd wait for him at the top of the stair, sitting close together with Tom in the middle, his knees jigging up and down.

They resembled each other so much, my children, but of course they were nothing the same. Willie was worried all his life; that look he had when he was born never really left him. As a baby he would lie quite still and stare at the cracked ceiling,

and he was slow to talk, so different from his sister. Sadie was
not yet a year when she looked at me and said, *Mama,* and I can
still see the dress she was wearing, still feel the chill in my fingertips, for it was the end of a cold winter. I scooped her up and
held her so tight. I often thought, when Sadie was small, how I
had my own mother until I was almost three. I thought of the
things Sadie and I said to each other, of the shape of our days,
the little games we played, and I couldn't believe that if I were to
die, she would keep nothing of that. What Tom said first I don't
remember; he made noise from the minute he was born, and
at some point it turned into words. Without the cordial I don't
know how I would have lived through his first year, how either
of us would.

Carbolic Acid	gtt xxxij
Chlorate of Potash	ʒiij
Glycerine	ʒiij
Water	ʒv

William loved Sadie, she was always his special girl, but he
had such pride in his sons. Sometimes he had to go back to the
Works for some reason and would take them with him, Tom in
his arms and Willie trotting beside, and he let them sit on his
high stool and once Mr. Keele was there, and said they were fine
fellows. Sometimes on a Sunday he took them down to the
docks to see the big ships while Sadie and I swept out our rooms,
and coming home Tom said he was going to be a sea captain and
sail all around the world. On Saturdays William always had
something in his pockets and the one after that he had a sailor's
cap for Tom; it was big and drooped over his left eye but he
didn't take it off for weeks, not even to sleep. *How much did that
cost,* I said, but he said what he always did, that it wasn't my con-

cern. When we married I thought we might live in my father's house but it seemed he had borrowed against it, and had other debts besides, so there was nothing left. When William was moved to the office he got a little rise but most of it went on our bigger rooms and he still wore the cracked, shined boots he'd had when I met him. But on Saturdays there was always something in his pockets and sometimes things I knew we couldn't afford. A spyglass for Willie, three sheets of fine paper for Sadie. Once I said, sharpish, that maybe we could have meat twice in the week if there was so much money to spare.

. . .

Bessie had a growth that started to eat away at her from the inside, and from such a big woman she turned into the frailest thing. I went to see her when I could but it was difficult, trailing three small children, the long trip across town. After she died her daughters came and took everything, even the silver spoon she meant for me to have. It was like my own mother dying all over again, and this time I was grown and knew it. Sorrow like a weight I felt on my shoulders.

I am your family, William said. *We are your family.* Pointing to the room where the children slept. *We are everything you need.*

> . . . a warm bath, then bleeding, next tartar emetic every 15 minutes until symptoms of collapse are produced, giving brandy if the prostration becomes too great.

The building where we lived was mostly families, except for a few like Old John, all on his own, who roared and shook his walking stick when anyone stepped in his way. The children played in the courtyard all day and into the evening and the sound of their chanting, their calling, was like the sound of hooves, of cart wheels rumbling by, so constant I only noticed when it stopped. Sadie played there most days, though William didn't know. He thought she would pick up all kinds of things; said, *We're not like them.* In some ways it was true, and I thanked God every Saturday night when Harold Ashe came stumbling home, tripping on the steps on the landing, cursing and banging on the door because his fingers had become too thick to fit in his pocket for his key. The thumps and crashes. All the women on their own with sickly children or just too many, hunched over washtubs with cracked red hands.

But in some ways we were just like them, a family with young children and never enough money. It's no life for a child, cooped up in three small rooms when the sun is shining and voices float up the stairwell. Willie played in the courtyard too, though mostly he liked to sit in his own corner, building things from the scraps of wood and brick that William sometimes brought home. Once I was carrying Tom to the shop and I stopped to tell Sadie I'd be soon back. The children were all in a line, ten of them or twelve, with their arms down at their sides, jumping straight up in the air and one little girl watching, calling out who jumped highest. And every time it was Willie, my Willie, with his eyes closed and his arms stiff at his sides, jumping higher and higher, jumping straight into the air. *He's the fastest runner too,* Sadie said. *He can run like the wind, he wins all the races.* How strange it was, that I hadn't known that about my own child, that I hadn't known that Willie, with his calm and thoughtful way, could run like the wind. And though I'd been with my children every day of their lives, though I'd loved them more than I could imagine, I suddenly saw them in a new way, saw things I'd been missing because I'd never thought to look for them, because maybe I'd never really looked, thinking I already knew.

. . .

Sadie was desperate to go to school and William wanted her to go to Mrs. Cook's, half a mile away. He said he would get the money, he said she should be patient, wait another year, but Sadie, usually so obedient, didn't stop asking. Though he never raised his voice, sometimes he got quite cross. I waited until he'd finished his meal, set down his fork, wiped his beard. *It's so important to her,* I said. And he said what he said to Sadie, that she deserved better than the little school down the road, the children fighting in the street. I reminded him of what he often said, that he'd still be toting bricks if he hadn't learned to figure so well, and he said he didn't deny it, but it was surely more important for a boy, who would one day have a family to support. *We can't know,* I said. And I said that something could happen to us, that Sadie could be left to make her own way in the world, to take care of her brothers, that surely she'd have a better chance of that with an education. And I asked if he could bear to think of her scrubbing clothes, or minding ten babies in a tiny room. *A year,* William said, *maybe ten months, and I'll have the money for Mrs. Cook's,* and I asked him if he remembered how long a year was, when he was a child, how long a month. *I've never asked you for a thing,* I said, *but I'm asking this now,* and in the end he agreed.

Hot irritating applications should be applied to the throat extending to the ears on each side. 2 or 3 layers of flannel saturated with a mixture of kerosene, collodium, turpentine etc. should suffice. Pork and mustard also answer the purpose very well. Also oil of turpentine 3 times per day in teaspoonful doses, mixed with spirits of ether.

I made Sadie a new dress from a skirt of mine that wasn't too worn, and we bought a slate and the night before William brought home a handful of ribbons for her hair and left them on the table for her to find when she woke. She already knew her numbers and letters, could read some words and write all our names, but the first day she got her knuckles rapped for the shape of her *A* and I feared that William was right. But it never happened again, or if it did she didn't say, and soon the teacher had her helping the slowest ones, as she was so far ahead. I missed her terribly, until I got used to it. Lunchtimes were short but when she came home in the afternoons she hugged us all, and then sat down at the table with Willie and showed him what she'd learned that day. Some days it wasn't much; *I helped the little ones with their letters all day,* she'd say, or, *The bigger boys broke a bench and had to be whipped, and that took a long time.* There were days when she'd learned a new poem and she'd stand very still and recite it with her hands folded in front, like they were taught, and her eyes half closed. Sometimes they were poems that I knew and I was sorry again that my books had been sold, for I knew how she would have loved them. Her handwriting was beautifully clear and she liked to leave notes for her father to find, writing *Mr. William Heath, Esq.* with a great flourish, and drawing hearts in the corners.

What Willie liked best was the arithmetic Sadie taught him, and although his numbers were shaky in the writing he usually had the right answer, and often just by figuring in his head. *You must get that from your father,* I told him, and he was very like William with his serious air, his way of speaking only when something needed saying. Sometimes I thought I saw two faint lines between his eyebrows. He was like William too in caring to be clean, and I never had to remind him to wash when he came in from outside. The thing William hated most about the brick-yard was the way the dust settled on his hair, on every bit of skin, the dirt always under his fingernails. When he began to work in the office he let his fingernails grow rather long, and I supposed it was because he could.

· · ·

Charlie Ashe said his mother couldn't leave her bed and when I opened the door of their room the smell was foul, and Annie barely able to open her eyes. I sent for the doctor and whether because of him or in spite of him, she got better. Sadie asked me, *Can women be doctors too?* and I said I thought there were a few. *That's what I'll be,* she said, and she wanted to practice on us, give us medicine, and I mixed up a little sugar water. *But medicine has to taste bad,* she said, and I said we would pretend, and she gave us spoonsful of sugar water and we all made terrible faces. Sometimes she bandaged Tom using bits from the rag bag, around his head and one arm and the other leg tied to splints. Tom who could rarely sit still, I was surprised, but he said she gave him sixpence. *Where did you get sixpence,* I said, and she said it was from William, for doing so well at school.

My Tom had lovely fair curls and the longest eyelashes and a way of looking at you that made it hard to stay cross. If there was a crash of something breaking or an angry mother at the door, that would be Tom. He'd never been able to sit still, and though he was small for his age he would climb anything, try anything, fight even the biggest boy. He was always coming in with bruises and scrapes and I thought sometimes that if we lived in the country, if we had all that space where he could run and run. I wondered what kind of man he'd make, with his quick temper, his fidgets. But for all the trouble he caused he was a kind boy, always standing up for the picked-on ones, always ready to laugh, and I thought that he'd be all right.

· · ·

A man was giving a talk on Canada; William saw the notice on his way home and had to stand at the back of the crowded room. *It's the place for us,* he said. *I wish you could have heard.* I said I had no intention of living in a cabin in the woods but he said I had the wrong idea, that we could go to one of the towns or a city, smaller than here and cleaner, everything new, even the air. Plenty of work for a man like him, he'd asked about that, and the kind of opportunities that would never come his way where he was. *And for the children,* he said, *just think of that, they could do anything there, be anything; it's the future.* I said we could never afford the passage, and he said he'd worry about that. It was the most he'd said to me in months. William wasn't much of a talker and I didn't think I was either; I thought that was one way we were suited to each other. When we married I thought it would be difficult, to live so close with someone, but of course I had days to myself and in truth he was easier than my father, keeping his things tidy and taking off his boots at the door. I told him things, all kinds of things, lying in the dark with my mother's quilt over us, and he asked me questions but rarely answered mine. *I don't remember,* he would say, or, *I don't know,* or, *I never think of it.* When the children were born my days were filled with talk and I babbled to them long before they could answer. William came home late with a pain behind his eyes; he took off his boots and ate his meal and sometimes read a newspaper he'd picked up. In the mornings he drank his tea while I roused the children and brushed and scrubbed them, cutting bread and tying laces and sometimes days went by when we hardly said a word to each other, when he was gone from my thoughts the moment he closed the door.

I was always tired, slept like a stone unless one of the children called out, and then feeling my way back to the bed I was sometimes startled, touching William's hard shoulder. Once I dreamed that I opened my eyes but was still in the dark; I couldn't move, couldn't speak. I could hear quiet voices, could hear children crying, my children, and I tried with all my might to reach for them, to make a sound. And then it felt like I sat up with a roar, but William didn't stir, so perhaps the roaring was somewhere in the dream I'd left. The room was pearly with the light of the first dawn and I could see then, I could move, but I didn't sleep again.

> After having previously evacuated the stomach with ipecac, cauterize the fauces and the trachea with a strong solution of nitrate of silver, by means of a probang pushed into it while the epiglottis is held with a finger of the left hand. Repeat the operation every few hours. In addition a 50% solution of chloral hydrate may be applied with a hair pencil every half hour. The pain caused by it is sometimes severe.

William had no use for religion, and although I had been a churchgoer all my life, when we moved across town it was too far to go back on my own and the new church just wasn't the same. I gradually got out of the habit, though I was never quite easy about it. Still, it was nice to have a late breakfast all together on a Sunday, and if the weather was fine we sometimes went walking. One Sunday the blossoms were on the trees and William was in good spirits, teasing the children and stopping to rest a hand on my shoulder. Sadie said her throat was scratchy and he said a picnic by the river would fix her right up and we set off all together, Tom riding on William's shoulders and Sadie carrying our old blanket, me with the eggs I'd been saving and some bread and a bottle of water.

2 leeches are sufficient for a child a year old, 4 for three years & so on. Place them on the trachea when you can watch them, but on the sternum if compelled to leave.

At first Willie held my hand but some boys he knew were standing at the corner and I let him go. He raced on ahead and ran back to us, panting and saying, *Was I faster this time? This time?* It was the first real day of spring and the streets were filled with families like us and the men touched their caps, the women smiled, and we wished each other good day. Tom babbled on about all he could see far ahead and Willie ran faster and faster, Sadie sang her walking song and there were blossoms on the trees. I thought that any day now I would feel the quickening, and moving through that soft air, I counted my blessings.

Diphtheria is the most insidious of the acute diseases, and children under ten years are particularly vulnerable to infection. Despite all efforts and the best care and treatment, some families will lose every one.

LOCKET

SHE POLISHES IT only when she is alone in the house, and even then behind the closed door of the bedroom. As if it's something that must remain secret, the locket she has worn for years beneath the buttons of her dress, an oval lump that anyone might notice, although no one ever has. Not even William, who gave it to her when they were first married, fastened it around her neck, touched the etched, twining leaves with the tip of his finger. Told her that it was the first gift he had ever given. William must know how she wears it now but he has never said, another part of the silence between them that at times seems as vast as the ocean they crossed, sailing away from their first life together.

When she takes the locket off she feels the empty space near her heart, and as she gets older and her fingers thicken and stiffen it takes longer to do the clasp again, longer to feel that first cold touch, to feel it begin to warm. She has seen ornate brooches, pinned to women's jackets, and in the Reverend's parlor a design of flowers and leaves under glass. Things made with stiff, woven strands of a loved one's hair, twisted into unnatural shapes, things that make her shudder. She felt faint in the parlor, watching Mrs. Toller's nimble fingers flitting over the tea tray, and even though there was something wounded in the brown eyes, even though she knew that something was about to be said, she had to leave, apologies spilling out as she fumbled with the door. Outside her head was spinning and filled with things she didn't want to see. There is a black space in her mind that has oozed and spread and covered those terrible days. The only thing she really remembers is Annie Ashe placing a tiny paper packet into her empty hand, opening it just enough to show the three curls of hair, so small, so soft, each tied with a bit of thread.

The boat from Liverpool was filled with children, calling out to each other in their clear high voices. Once a little girl sat beside her on a bolted bench; they looked out at the empty sea and she stroked the child's hair, whispered to her, and the child leaned into her with a small sigh. Then a long-nosed woman came, then William came, and led her away with his strong arm hooked through hers. She lay on her berth, the flutter of new life so faint that even though she knew it was wrong, she could move her mind away from it, pretend it wasn't there at all. When the boat was finally still, at the dock in the new world, she opened the paper packet, used a hat pin to tease the thread-bound wisps into the oval space inside the locket. Snapped it shut.

There were hard times after, and times that were not so hard, and she dressed herself and brushed her hair, loved her children, the living and the lost, loved her husband. But none of it felt like her own life. Sometimes she remembered the long-nosed woman on the ship, leading the little girl away. Remembered seeing the child's step hesitate, skip, faster or slower, as she tried to match the pace. That was as close as Naomi could come to the way it felt, her life now lived in that hesitation, in that stuttering moment, trying to match up, to slide back into something, an easy gait. Thinking of it that way didn't change anything, but she felt a little better knowing there was a way to describe it, her life, if there was ever a reason to, ever a need.

WEDNESDAY'S CHILD—1888

THREE PEOPLE LOVE me in this world, and that should be enough. One is my mother, and I will never leave her. One is my sister, who is the best of us, the hope of us. Like in the garden. The last is my father, who takes care of us, but doesn't always see.

There are families in church with children like steps on a stair, and babies, and grandmothers in black bonnets. And there are people who have no one at all. No one could love the tattered woman who mumbles outside Malley's tavern, and Mr. Envers used to set down his mug of tea and tell my mother it was a terrible thing to outlive everyone, to be all alone. When we first came to this town Rachel had to write an essay for Miss Alice, about her family. Parents and grandparents, where they came from, what they did. There was a silence at the dinner table and then my father said, *That's no one's business; no one has any right to ask that.* Rachel said that she had to, that it was an essay, and he gave her a look that he didn't often give, and was silent for the rest of the meal. Later, in the kitchen, my mother told about her own parents, and what she knew of theirs. A ship our great-grandfather had owned, and how he was lost. A curved sword someone had brought back from war. She said it was all true but her voice sounded like a story, like the stories she used to tell when she pulled the covers up over us, smoothed them with her hand.

They came in the evening, in the dark. A brisk knocking at the door. I was at the foot of the stair; my father, in his shirtsleeves, opened it, letting in a whisper of dying leaves along with a rush of cold, sharp-scented air.

Wednesdays at eleven o'clock I go across the road to Dr. Robinson, and I see the week like a hill now, sloping up to a peak and then sliding down again. At first it was like waves building and crashing over my head. People on the street, the dark hallway, the unfamiliar room and the questions. He asked my mother things, asked me things, that were so private I didn't even have words for them. But now I know what things look like, behind the gleaming door. Dr. Robinson examines my tongue, touches my face with his clean fingers, pulling down the skin beneath my eyes. Holds my wrist and counts without seeming to count. He told my mother that she didn't always need to come with me, that he could send for her if need be, just across the road. The first time I went alone she watched me from the front porch, and each time I looked back she waved her hand. When I returned she was still there, sitting on the outside chair. She smoothed my hair back and gave me her sad smile and I told her it was fine, that the laughing girl had been there for a little while.

He stepped out onto the front porch, closed the door, and I couldn't hear a thing they were saying. Only Rachel's happy voice from the kitchen, where she was helping my mother. I couldn't hear the words they were saying but it was so strange, this knock in the dark, my father stepping out in his shirtsleeves, that I didn't continue up. I sank down onto the third stair and waited, smoothing my skirts over my knees.

They were there as long as I can remember, there in the room where mist trailed by the window, in the darker, noisier room. The jumping boy and the laughing girl. Not every moment, not every day, but enough to be without surprise. Sometimes I talked to them but they never answered, and I don't know that they even saw me. The way I saw them hard to explain, something like a thought that ravels away when you try to catch hold of it. Sometimes words came into my head and I spoke them out loud; once my mother said, *Who are you talking to, Lily? Are you talking to someone?* When I said, *The jumping boy,* she dropped the plate she was holding; it smashed with a terrible sound and bits lay jagged on the floor. Her voice when she spoke so slow and careful, but with something humming beneath. She asked, and I told her how the boy jumped straight in the air, so high, his light hair flopping. How the girl sometimes had smudges where she'd touched her cheek with her fingers. I was still in the bed and though my mother's voice was slow and soft, it frightened me a little, something did. Just the two of us there; maybe I was very young, Rachel not yet born. I wanted to tell her about the children and yet I didn't, and I worked my finger in the hole in the brown blanket, making it bigger, but my mother didn't tell me to stop. I had never questioned, never thought before that maybe they were only mine. The jumping boy, the laughing smudgy-cheeked girl, and sometimes the other who was just a streak of color at the edge of my looking.

My mother asked me questions, in the soft voice that soothed, with the hum beneath that frightened. What did they look like, what were they doing, were they happy or sad. When I asked, she said they were children she knew once. And when I asked where they were now, she just said, *Gone.* And then she did a strange thing. She walked toward the bed, the broken shards crunched beneath her feet, and with all her clothes on, even her shoes, she crawled under the bedclothes and put her arms about me, and we both fell asleep again, even though it was already day.

There was someone else, but only Constable Street came in with my father when the door opened, the tip of his nose red. Miss, he said with a nod, but my father walked by as if he didn't even see me, fetched his coat. His face wiped clean of everything, smooth as stone.

The graves in the churchyard are marked by straight standing stones, and although the church is not old, there are so many. Mothers and fathers and children, whole families, sometimes, buried together. Rachel and her friends play a game, hold their breath when they walk by on the way to the gaping doors of the church. When I fainted there on the steps it was just like the other times, the buzzing getting louder, muffling the voices around me. The yellow mesh becoming denser and denser before my eyes until it closed in completely, blotted everything out. My mother felt the tug on her arm as I started to slide down but she wasn't strong enough, and when I opened my eyes I screamed at all the faces, bending over me. Dr. Robinson put his fingers on my wrist and asked if this had happened before, and I heard Rachel say that it happened almost every day, but I forgave her. That is how I came to sit on a chair in his office the first time, the scratch of his pen and everyone seizing on the word that he gave me, as if it said everything, as if it could hold every part of me, each dark part. Now I sit in that chair every Wednesday and things are checked, and then we talk. I've told him about the pebbles I carry in my mouth, but not about the other things.

My mother came from the kitchen, wiping her hands, and the constable nodded to her too, looked down at his shuffling feet. He said there was just a little matter to clear up, and my father said nothing at all, as the front door closed behind them.

I was born in Halifax, where the ship first docked; my mother says there was no money to go any farther. She says there was one tiny room, that we lived there for years, maybe three, maybe four, but I don't remember. Only swirls of mist and the sound of gulls, and maybe a game that we played, my mother sitting with her face in her hands. My father worked in an office on the docks, but he had to leave. We sailed up the river to Montreal, and those same gulls wheeled around our boat.

When Rachel asked, my mother said it was nothing. Some confusion, some little problem at the business, perhaps, and Rachel went lightly up to bed. I wondered why two constables would walk across town in the dark, for nothing.

In the evenings Rachel does her lessons at the kitchen table, and when she's finished she sometimes draws pictures of houses, of trees, on pieces of paper my mother saves for her. My father brought home a blotter, tucked under his coat, for the surface of the table is uneven, scarred and gouged by people we've never known. Rachel has made up stories about them, the families who walked through the rooms that are now ours, who ate their meals here, sat in these chairs. One family she calls the Whippets; they have two wild boys named Joshua and David. The deepest gouge on the table was made by David Whippet, with a pocketknife he was given for his birthday, and he was sent to his room for twenty-one days. Now when something is broken or spilled, my father says, *Which Whippet did that?*

I wonder about the families, the real families, and where they've gone. Marks of their anger, their errors, the only things we have to know them by. Walking toward the mouth of the church we have to pass the standing stones and I think how they may die before me, my father and my mother. Rachel must have her own life, tend our memories but nothing else. Mrs. Toller went to bed with a bottle of laudanum; I heard my father tell my mother. And a man named Meyer was found hanging in a barn. When I open my eyes in the morning there's always a moment when I wonder if it's a good thing.

My mother and I sat in the little front room that was filled, like the whole house, with things other people had left behind. The worn spot on the arm of the settee where she sat sewing, the spot rubbed bare by a stranger's hand. The needle flashed as she raised it, pulling the thread tight. She jabbed her finger and crumpled the white shirt to the floor. Then bent to pick it up again, smoothed it on her lap.

Dr. Robinson counted my pulse, checked my heart, looked in my eyes, my mouth. He asked questions, so many questions.

When I slept, what I ate, about my monthlies. All these my mother answered. Then he said that I had a condition, that there was a name for it. The name was *chlorosis,* and he wrote it down on a thick piece of creamy paper. The scratch of the pen drowned out by a raised voice from beyond the door, a woman's voice, chiding a servant. Sound of something that might have been a slap. He looked up at that but said nothing. Passed the paper to my mother and leaned back in his chair, hands on the edge of the desk. Loose threads, a button missing on his vest.

He told my mother that he'd been reading about this green sickness lately, that it was not uncommon in girls my age, that there were things that could be done. I meant to listen, but found I hadn't. Realized, when he stood up, that I'd been staring, just staring at the dangling stray threads, the place where a button belonged.

And is it better or worse, to know that there's a name? Things I felt long before I knew the words for them. Things change when you put a name to them, but they don't disappear. Just change.

My father seemed pleased with the word, asked each day if I'd walked, if I'd rested, if I'd taken the Blaud's pills. He said if it was to be meat every day then I should have it, and my family sat around me with their pale plates, potatoes and cabbage, a slice of bread. My mother knew how hard it was; meat, if I must eat it, I like burned black, hard like a stone in my mouth, bitter like the taste of Rachel's charcoal stick. A bit of chicken I could bear, not easily, but I could bear it, but the bloody taste of beef was an agony, though I cut the pieces as small as I could, made motions with my jaw and tried to swallow them straight down. They sat at the table day after day, my plate half full while theirs were wiped clean. Telling their bits of news over my bowed head as if there was nothing else they needed to do, nowhere else to be. The three people who love me in this world.

We sat and listened to the ticking of someone else's clock, to the wind picking up outside. My mother said she didn't know what was wrong. She told me instead about the look of my father's boots when they first met, a story I thought I'd heard before. I stood and pushed aside the curtain a little; there was a high, cold moon and I could see the fallen leaves skittering away in the dark.

My mother's hands are always red and sore and with all the cleaning and washing when we came to the new house they got worse, her fingers covered in raw spots where the swollen skin had cracked and split. Some days I had to do her buttons. Before she went to sleep she smeared her hands with a thick grease, and then she had to lie on her back with her arms straight, palms up outside the covers. Once my father came home with a little pot of cream he'd bought at Mr. Marl's pharmacy and he sat across from her in the kitchen, working it in, kneading from her wrist to the tip of her fingers, stroking her palm, pressing her knuckles.

Her sore hands made my father angry. He said we should hire a servant; he said she shouldn't have to do so much, with only me to help, but she just said, *Oh, William.* Money was still owed to someone for something; I'd heard them talking about that behind their closed door. And even I knew that if Rachel's only dresses were mine made over, if we had to use the tea leaves twice, and sometimes twice again, then there was no money to hire a servant. But my father said soon there would be, said this was a town where he could climb higher and higher. Already in charge of the Sunday school, and there'd been talk of him joining a club. He said that we should go out more, make calls; he said that was how things worked here, how connections were made. And my mother said she would, but just now there was so much to do.

It was strange to hear my father talk that way. In the cities we had lived in people on the same stair knew us a little but mostly, as he used to say, we could keep ourselves to ourselves. In Toronto each time the fat woman came with her basket he brushed by her in the doorway, even when she asked him to stay. Leaving my mother to thank her for the things she brought, to answer the questions, all the questions. The fat woman wanted to know all our business, writing in her little book. She spoke kind words but her lips had a way of folding, her eyes looking everywhere. She told my mother about other families she visited, where the husband was ill or paralyzed, or just gone. She said that my mother was lucky, that her man was perfectly healthy, that there must be something he could do. Buildings to be built, streetcar tracks to be laid. As if it were all his fault. Still, she was the one who read Mr. Marl's advertisement, who learned that his bookkeeper had recently died. My father polished his boots and walked to the station; he was gone two days and when he came back he brought a posy of white flowers for my mother, a piece of beef, wrapped in greased paper. He said all our troubles were over.

Behind me, my mother said, Your father loves us. *Said,* It will be fine, go up to bed. *I thought then of safe places, how they had come to be this little white house, the yard with its high board fence. Dr. Robinson's office when the door is closed and maybe, just maybe, the streets I know in this town. How suddenly they were all shriveling back down to a dot, to the room where my mother sat, to the space on the cushion beside her. How she was sending me away.*

Something happened in Halifax, something happened in Montreal, and maybe in England before. My father knows; my mother may. In Toronto he lost his job, though at first he didn't say. One morning he forgot to take his bread and my mother fretted, saying she knew he wouldn't spend money for something from a stall, and she took it to the factory for him. We went early to bed that night while they spoke in the other room, and Rachel whispered that she'd already known, that she'd seen him one day when she took a different way home from school, sitting on a bench, staring down at his hands. Terrible days came after.

The children were everywhere in my room; they were chanting a rhyme and although I could hear every word I couldn't catch hold of any of them, just the echo they left in the air. The darting child left trails of color, made me dizzy, and for the first time in months I reached under my mattress for the bone-handled knife, rolled down my stocking.

Rachel recites the kings and wars of England, she knows *amo amas amat*, and all the capitals of Europe. Perhaps if I'd gone to school. My mother saying no to my father, in a hard voice. Saying, *You **know** why.* She taught me to read from the Bible, her own mother's name written inside in faint, spiked letters, and from the newspaper when we had one. That was easier, the letters larger, the words more familiar. But not as beautiful as the Bible, as the words in the Bible. When my mother read from the Bible I felt as if I were in a green field, with sun on my face, or sitting by a stream, hearing water over smooth stones. Though I hadn't done either of those things. It wasn't like in church, not like hearing Reverend Toller; he read different parts.

Darkness and screaming, the plagues of Egypt, the sufferings of Job. Reverend Toller's Bible was filled with terrible tests. Abraham on the mountain with his knife raised, and Isaac bound tight, looking into his eyes.

My father said it wasn't enough to be able to read, to write my name. In Toronto, before the men took our furniture, Mr. Envers used to come, already unwinding his long, greasy scarf when my mother opened the door. He was no taller than she was, his hair stuck flat to his head and his beard stained yellow, tumbling down his front. The little bundle of books, tied with a bit of rope. One of the books had maps and he opened it to the middle and touched the page, his fingers yellowed like his beard, the nails almost as long as my father's. *This is England,* he said, *where you are from, the Atlantic Ocean your parents crossed. This is Halifax, where you were born, and Montreal. Toronto, where we sit now.*

And all the words brought pictures, a forest and a vast stretch of ruffled water, gulls wheeling and dancing, a cobbled street slick with rain. I couldn't see how that happened, as if the pictures were somehow folded into a dot on a page, like a bud that's waiting, that looks like nothing until it opens. There was something I almost understood then, understood in the same way I see the leaping boy, from the corner of my eye. There was something I almost had, but Mr. Envers didn't notice. Instead he picked up Rachel's ball from the floor and said, *This is the Earth, the North Pole and the South. This is England, here, and Canada, America. And this round Earth spins and spins, so quickly we cannot feel it.* Then my mind slid away, for that I couldn't grasp at all.

Mr. Envers came through the winter and the spring and his voice was hoarse, not much above a whisper, and sometimes he coughed until tears ran down his cheeks. Then my mother would make him a cup of tea if she had any leaves, and he would tell her about boys he had taught, now doctors and lawyers and one in the government. How they'd never forgotten him. The lessons got shorter and shorter, the time with the cup longer. Once he asked my mother if I was good with a needle.

Then Rachel called out and I went to her, across the dark hall. She was sitting up in bed, and in the bit of moonlight that slipped through the top of her window her hair was a sooty tangle, her eyes deep in her face. What was the noise? *she said.* A bang, a loud bang, it woke me. Hush, *I said,* there was no noise, no noise; it must have been a dream. *She sank back down onto her thin pillow and I sat on the edge of the bed beside her, held her hand until it slipped away from mine.*

This is the first real house we've lived in, all the rooms just ours. The kitchen and the three bedrooms. The front room with its heavy brown furniture, the privy in the back. When my father brought us to it, helped my mother down from the wagon that had carried us from the station, she clasped her hands together, rested her chin on them like someone praying, and smiled and smiled. Not her sad smile, but a different one. Inside my father wound the clock on the wall, and when it started to tick he put a hand on her shoulder and said that this was our real beginning. She took his hand and lifted it to her lips, and Rachel ran upstairs and down, through the front door and out the back, and came in again, saying, *There's a yard, is it ours? And a little tree right in the middle.*

The yard is ours, with a fence along one side, and along the back where the laneway runs. On the other side a mass of bushes, covered with red berries at the end of summer. A tree that's not much taller than Rachel, and a little shed that my father said was for chickens. He came home one day with three in a wicker basket, and a small rooster with a drooping comb that Rachel named Simon Peter.

The chickens were for me, my father said, for me to take care of. I never said, but I didn't like anything about them. The greedy way they went after the food I scattered, and they pecked at me, at each other, and squawked and chased Simon Peter away when he came too close. Some days there were no eggs at all and my father went back to the market, thinking he'd been cheated. He came home with another rooster, a big, strutting fellow he called Lord Bray, and the hens didn't peck at him, didn't flap him away, they all lay down for him. Simon Peter was for the pot but Rachel cried and pleaded and we kept him too, until one morning I found him in a little ruffled heap by the canes, Lord Bray with blood on his beak. Simon Peter's feathers swirled all around the back step where my mother and I plucked him, and we tried to gather them all up again. When asked, my mother said that he had flown away over the high fence, and I could tell that it pained her, watching Rachel lift the fork to her mouth.

My room was empty and silent now but still I couldn't settle, and when I heard the front door I took my shawl and sat at the top of the stair. I heard my father say, Nothing to fret about, *and he said that Mr. Lett had posted bail, that it was so late because they had to wait for the Odd Fellows meeting to finish. He asked my mother for a cup of tea, and as they moved to the kitchen my father said that he had to appear in court at noon, that it was a misunderstanding, that it would all be fine. Then the scrape of the stove being stirred, the rattle of the kettle, covered their voices. Only once, my mother saying,* What will become of us? *Saying,* I can't bear it, to start again.

My mother thought we should grow our own vegetables, now that we had a yard, and my father turned over a square of earth, held up his own red hands at the end of the day and said he'd been too long in an office. He made a low fence around our garden, to keep the chickens out, and we planted potatoes and carrots, a few sweet peas. When the work was done Rachel made a sign for each row, and we all stood together in our own yard. The light was thick and golden, the sun moving down; we looked back to the house that was all ours, the brown door and the step where my mother and I sometimes sat, and that moment went on and on.

We checked every day, watched the green shoots push through the soil, more and more of them, and when we thought it was time my mother and I went out with a bowl to pull some carrots for our dinner. But the carrots we pulled were tiny, stunted things, some just a tangle of roots; my mother pulled more and more, all the same, and she put her hand to her cheek, leaving a muddy print, saying, *What did I do? What did I do wrong?*

The green-eyed woman who looked after Mr. Cowan next door was hanging out clothes; she must have heard us for she pushed through the bushes and came to look. *Didn't you thin them at all?* she said, and she told my mother that she should have pulled the seedlings, many of them, told her that was the only way the others could grow straight and strong. *Have you never grown a carrot before?* she said, and my mother said no, that she'd never had a bit of earth before. Her cheeks red, as if she'd said a shameful thing. *Never mind,* the woman said. *You*

can try again next year; next year you'll know. And she said that
Mr. Allen had a few nice carrots left to sell, that no one would
have to know. But my mother said that wouldn't be honest, and
the woman gave a little shrug, a smile. All we'd gathered just
made one small serving on my father's plate, but he said they
were the best he'd ever tasted.

*I must have fallen asleep, leaning at the top of the stair, for the
next thing I knew was my father's hand on my shoulder, his voice
whispering,* Go back to bed now Lilian, go to sleep now. *I heard
him close the door of their room, heard his cufflinks chink in the little china dish, heard the creak of the bed as he sat on it. But I don't
know that anyone really slept in our house that night. Only Rachel,
deep in her dreams. There were footsteps and creakings and mur-
murings, and if they stopped there were other sounds that dragged
me back. A dog barking somewhere close, a tree moaning. The clock
ticked louder than it ever did in the day, as if it was ticking right
inside my head.*

Days I stay in bed Rachel often sits with me, not asking me to
talk but just keeping me company, telling me things. Jokes and
stories, what she learned at school, things she thought about.
Like the days we used to share a bed, when she was two and I
was seven, how she curled up against me, how she chattered and
patted my face until one of us slept. Not long ago, sitting on the
edge of my bed, her face hard to make out in the rain-colored
room, she told me that Miss Alice had read a poem by Mr. Tennyson, that all the girls had tears in their eyes. And then she said
wasn't it a strange thing to cry? The way it sneaks up, the way
you know it's coming but you can hardly ever stop it. The way
your throat goes thick, something happens in your stomach. I

didn't say, but I realized that's the way I feel. Almost all of the time.

My father's eyes were red-rimmed and the ends of his trousers dark with damp; he said he'd woken early and been out walking. My mother's cheek scored as if she'd slept on something harsh instead of her own clean pillow. We blinked at each other around the kitchen table as if we'd just come out of some dark cave, as if we couldn't bear the morning light. Even Rachel eating quietly, looking a question that she didn't ask.

One Sunday after church my father said, *Let's walk a little; it's such a beautiful day*. He held out his arm to my mother, and after a moment she took it. We were always near the last to leave, not liking the crush at the door, so the footbridge was empty when my father led us there. And it was a beautiful day, patches of snow still on the ground, especially beneath the trees at the edge of the river, but the sun was high and the air was soft, our coats unbuttoned. Rachel skipped ahead, her long hair lifting and floating, until my mother called her back, her voice a little sharp. Perhaps because she had to speak loudly to be heard over the rumbling water. It had been a sudden thaw, the river running high and fast, and already two boys had been lost. We didn't know them, we hardly knew anyone, but my mother wept for them all the same.

There came a point, near the middle of the bridge, when my heart began to race. The way the boards moved, just a little, beneath our feet, and I wasn't sure that I could carry on. But the way back was just as far; my feet slowed and I could no longer hear the rushing river, my heart thumping and thumping in my ears, in every part of my body. My parents walking slowly ahead, and Rachel just ahead of them, and I felt so strange that I wondered if I was dying, wondered if this was what it was like, if this was the moment when it was done. But I wasn't ready, and I had always believed I would be ready. It was a mistake and I had to move, before they were lost to me.

I looked at the back of the houses on the far side of the river, the secret side of the houses, and some of them had boats, had rowboats upside down near the water's edge, and I thought, *An upside-down boat will not hold anyone*. But with that thought came a sound like far-off laughter, and I found I was thinking of a woman in a long white dress, leaning back on faded cushions while someone rowed one of those boats. The blue one, maybe, that was almost the color of the sky. Rowing along the green river on a warm summer's day, with a parasol, perhaps, to shade her from the sun. Trailing her fingers in the water, and I knew how the water would feel, warm and silky. The trees along the riverbank were bare but I saw how they would be, in summer, in full dark leaf. And all the weeping willows, their branches curving down to make a sheltered place there on the riverbank, a place where a person could sit and be content. My heart slowed down and I could hear the churgling river again, as I looked at the place where I would sit, in summer, and watch a boat glide by with the tiniest splash of oars. I saw my father and Rachel walking hand in hand, almost at the other side, saw my mother had missed me, had turned and started back for me, and my feet moved again; I made my feet move.

On the far side the steps were splintered and worn but they were solid enough, and ahead of us, to the left, was the back of a yellow brick cottage, with a small sign in one window saying *Fine Photography*. My father said, *That's what we should do; we should have our photograph taken. What do you say, Naomi?* And Rachel said, *Can we do it now, right now?* Tugging at his hand, but he wasn't looking at her. He said my mother's name again, said, *To mark our new life. What do you say,* but all she said was that no one would be there on the Sabbath. He knocked at the little back door anyway, went round to the front, just a step from the narrow street, and finally the front door opened and there was a man with his hair all ruffled, his suspenders hanging looped at his sides. After he had closed the door again, my father said he would come back another day and arrange it all.

He was strange that day, my father, in such high spirits. He led us up a narrow, winding street that climbed the hill, as if he knew exactly where he wanted us to go. Though there were not so many houses as on our side of the river, they grew larger and larger as we reached the top of the climb. Enormous houses of red or yellow brick, of stone, some with turrets, with colored glass in the windows, with long verandas looking down on the river, looking down on the rest of the town. We came to a place with iron gates standing open, and he led us a little way up the curved drive. Another house with many chimneys, a glassed room built out on one side that had colored streaks, maybe birds, flitting behind the windows. *Mr. Marl's house,* my father said. *We shall have a house like that one day.* My mother said, *Oh, William,* but Rachel took it up, saying, *Really? Will we really?* My father said, *Of course we will,* and he stooped a little to put an arm around her shoulders, pointing out the windows, the rooms, asking her to choose which one would be hers. *We must go,* my mother said, plucking at his cuff. *What if someone comes and finds us?* My father said, *What if they do?* But he turned away all the same.

My father pushed back his chair, said he had no appetite, and he caught my mother's hand as she reached to take his plate and held it for a moment. Then he left the kitchen and we heard his footsteps going back and forth, back and forth, in the room above our heads. After I had watched Rachel cross the road to school he came down with his hat in his hands, said he had errands to do in town. My mother asked if he would get a few nails to fix the loose board on the chicken coop, but he said he would do it another day.

Dr. Robinson counts my heartbeats, looks in my mouth and my eyes. Once he tried the electric box; he gave me his own white handkerchief and said it was a shame that it had upset me. Said that he knew it would help, that we would try again, but not for a month or two. When I went home I still had the handkerchief crumpled in my hand; I washed it and pressed it and put it under my pillow so I wouldn't forget to take it back.

After the checking Dr. Robinson sits behind his desk, all his buttons sewn on. I sit in the chair and listen to him talk and it doesn't take so long now, for me to be able to stop staring at the toes of my shoes. He talks about how the treatment is working, how I am progressing, and it may be true, although there are always things I don't tell him. He asks how my mother likes the town, says that his own wife came from the city, as he did, that she found it difficult, at first. He talks about his son, Rachel's friend, how there are things a mother doesn't understand, things about being a boy. Sometimes when I raise my eyes he's not even looking at me, and sometimes he calls me someone else's name, but I never say. I know what it's like to have someone bring you back, even if it's done in the gentlest way.

Dr. Robinson reminds me of some nice type of dog, I don't know why. Maybe his brown eyes, the way his mustache droops over the corners of his mouth. The type of dog that would follow you everywhere, that would sleep on the end of your bed and only ask you to be kind to it. The type of dog that would always try to protect you, even when it couldn't. My mother had a dog like that once, in England. Its name was Blackie, and one day it ran into the road and was crushed by a brewer's cart. She never wanted another.

Dr. Robinson talks, and sometimes he stops and I can't even hear him breathing. I watch until he blinks his eyes, puts his hands on the desk, asks if I have any questions. One day I heard myself ask if it's true, that every life has a purpose. I didn't mean to ask it, I felt my face flush, I didn't know where to look, but he answered as if there was nothing strange in it, nothing strange in my speaking. He said he believes that's true, though a purpose can be many things. He told me about a promise he had to make once, to do no harm. Then he asked if I'd been thinking about that, asked what I think my purpose is. *Like the garden,* I said, and he waited for me to say more but I couldn't go on, my mind a jumble.

There was a bite in the air and the chickens pecked the ground around my feet, even though I'd scattered the grain in a wide circle. I was very tired, but I thought how it was Tuesday, and almost the top of the week. When I went back inside my mother was humming, heating up the stove and saying maybe she'd bake a cake later, if she had enough flour, saying we all needed something to cheer us up a little.

When my father polished his boots and came on the train without us, a man he met told him that Mr. Marl owns half the town. That may not be true, but his name is everywhere in Emden. On the big factory, the office block on the square, on the pharmacy and the jeweler's shop. In the newspaper. My father says Mr. Marl also started with nothing, says that is proof that anything is possible here, says this is our new beginning. He goes into the world each day, in a shirt we keep white and mended, in the boots he polishes himself. He returns from the world to the house, and the house is different when he does, when he is there. Just different. There are things he doesn't know, because we don't tell him, or because he doesn't see.

In the evenings my father sits in the armchair, the one with the stain no amount of scrubbing can remove, and while my mother sews he reads the paper out loud and the clock of our new life ticks and ticks. He reads the whole paper, even the deaths and marriages, and sometimes he will stop and say, *Another one gone, Lil, but plenty left for you. John Dawes, from church,* he said once. *Now there's a fine young man. Or Alec Lyon, steady and hardworking, and he'll inherit the mill.* As if all I had to do was decide, as if I would ever have a life like that, a normal life. He says things like that, and yet he was happy with the word, Dr. Robinson's word, and if he was happy with the word, that must mean he thought something needed to be explained. Maybe he sees more than he thinks, or more than he lets himself say. I know that my father loves me, but I don't know if he knows anything about me. I don't think he's ever held my hand in the street; I don't remember ever walking with him, just the two of us, alone.

When my father came back he had bought the nails after all and the sound of the hammer blows echoed, the chickens running in mad circles to the farthest corner of the yard. When he came in he rolled his shirtsleeves down and walked around the downstairs rooms, touching things but not picking them up, not even really

looking at them. My mother asked would I wash some windows
and I pumped the bucket as full as I could carry, gathered the rags.
But my father stopped me at the foot of the stair, said he needed a
piece of music for the Sunday school, a piece by Bach that Miss Al-
ice had, and would I go and fetch it now. I didn't say, but I won-
dered why he needed it then, with my hair wrapped up, my sleeves
already rolled. I wondered why Rachel couldn't bring it, why he
couldn't ask Rachel when she came home at noontime. He held the
door open and watched me on my way, the first time he'd been still
all morning. On the porch chair there was a package, wrapped in
brown paper and tied with string. A small package, strangely shaped,
like a lumpy letter L, and I wondered why he hadn't brought it
inside.

Rachel was born late, not like me, and my mother said that
was why she had such a mass of dark hair. She sometimes meets
my father after his work, and they walk through the town together. She can recite the kings and wars of England, all their
dates, and she draws the trees arching over the river, draws our
white house, draws Mr. Allen's store on the corner, with its
square sign, with its baskets of pears in front. She holds out her
hand under the table and takes my meat, sits on the end of my
bed when I'm too weary to rise. I watch her from the upstairs
window when she goes to school; there's a point where she dis-
appears, the angle of Mr. Allen's store, and I feel my heart
thump until I see her again, stepping up to Miss Alice's front
door. Every day the same.

Rachel is twelve now and women's things will happen to her,
but it won't be like me. One night in my bed the leaping boy put
his mouth to my ear and whispered, *Beware.* And I sat straight

up and realized that he had been gone, they had all been gone, and I had no idea how long. I thought of my mother, the waiting in her shoulders, and that's why I minded. The only thing I have to give her.

Rachel's friends told her that Will Toller has a crooked arm because his mother was frightened by a snake when she was carrying him, and she asked my mother if that was true. My mother looked even sadder, and she told Rachel that a mother and the child she carries are one flesh, that things can't help but be passed on.

Once outside the house I forgot my tiredness, forgot the strange, long night. The trees were standing still, red and orange against a clear blue sky, and though the air was cool on my cheeks, the sun was bright. Outside his store Mr. Allen was polishing apples on a little table and I thought of a pie my mother could make, thought of how one of those red apples would taste if I picked it up and bit into it. I thought that later I might take my walk by the river, instead of around and around the yard, and that thought carried me across the road to raise the knocker on the faded blue door, and I didn't even worry that it might be Mrs. Barnes who opened it, that I might have to look at her baffled gray eyes, repeat my sentence again and again.

Reverend Toller said there was evil about, in the shape of people who said they could talk to the dead. People who said that the dead appeared and rapped and spoke through them. Reverend Toller said that a woman in this very congregation had held such a gathering, invited such a person into her home. I wondered if my mother would have gone, if she'd known.

My mother's hands are cracked and sore and her hip aches, especially in rainy weather. She tells my father that she will make calls, join committees, but not just yet. I wonder that he doesn't know, what she can and cannot do. She goes to the shops in town, and if she will have a lot to carry, I go with her. People know her name, talk to her about the weather or the latest news. She smiles her sad smile and answers them, agrees about the sun or the clouds, *tsks* at the sad fate of Mrs. Toller. She is different in the shops, not completely, but a little. In her black dress, in her bonnet.

Our real life is in the house; it is only in the house that she hums sometimes, or sings a bit of one of my father's songs, or a hymn from church. In a house with five rooms there is always something to do, but sometimes she cuts a slice from a loaf that's just baked and we sit on the back step and tilt our faces to the sun. We are as close as thought, and even if she doesn't know the details of all my secrets, she knows their shape. Days I stay in bed I hear her footsteps moving through the house, climbing the stairs, and she strokes my forehead and whispers that she will take care of me always. We were one flesh, when she carried me.

My mother never asks about the children but there is a waiting in her shoulders, the way she bows her head, that eases when I tell her things. Sometimes, in an evil way, I fold my lips and say nothing; I don't know why. But not often. I watch her bend to the stove, watch her straighten up and rub at her sore hip, and everything lightens when I start to speak. She sinks into the chair across from me, the towel still in her hand, her eyes on my face. So many years we have done this, my hair growing longer, my mother's turning gray, but the children always the same.

It was Miss Alice who opened the door, as neat and gentle as always, and she had me come in while she searched out the music. The hallway was dark after the blue day but I saw a flicker of white, maybe the laughing girl flitting in and out of rooms. Through an open doorway on my left side I saw the pupils at the long school table, heads bent over their work. I saw Rachel's bent head, the parting I had made in her hair that morning, and then she looked up and smiled at me, we smiled at each other.

Years ago my mother told Mr. Envers that I was very good with a needle, and some days that is true. Other days my mind is a jumble and even her voice comes to me from far away. After the terrible days in Toronto my father brought my mother a posy of white flowers, and she put them in the mug with the picture of the woman in a boat and set them on the windowsill. On each stem there were small green buds, and day by day they changed. Lighter strips showing, growing wider, the green folds pushing apart so slowly. Two were like that, maybe three, though the others stayed tightly closed. We had to leave before I could see them completely open, but I suppose it might not have happened at all. The first flowers turning brown and limp around the edge of their petals. We took the mug but left the posy lying in a little puddle on the sill.

The package was gone from the outside chair and when I opened the door the house was silent, no sound of my mother's humming, not even the ticking clock. She had been mixing her cake when I left and there was a smell in the air, as if it had burned in the stove, and I wondered how I could have been gone so long. I started down the hall to find her, but my father called me from the top of the stair. I had the music in my hand, black notes dancing, and I held it out but he kept his hands behind his back, asked me to bring it up to him. The third stair cracked, like it always did, as I climbed toward my father. He stood very still, his hands behind his back, and I thought of the game he used to play with Rachel, wondered if it was finally my turn to guess which hand held the surprise.

GUN

S & W 32 D.A. 3½ INCH BARREL
New Model. Nickeled and Rubber stock. 5 Shot.
Weighs 13 oz., of elegant design and finest workmanship
    throughout.
Extra plating and Engraved handle, gives very fine
    "grip.". $8.00

DIRECTIONS FOR USE. *Half cock the arm;* raise the barrel
catch to its full height and tip the barrel forward as far as it
will go. Place the charges in the chambers and return the
barrel to its place, being sure to have the barrel catch down,
when the arm is ready for use.

While Carrying the Pistol Fully Charged, allow the hammer to
rest in the *safety catch.* After the first discharge, allow the

hammer to rest on the *exploded cartridge* until the next discharge, and so on until all are fired. Do not let your thumb slip off the hammer.

FORGIVENESS—1889

So here hath been dawning
Another blue day;
Think, wilt thou let it
Slip useless away?

—*Thomas Carlyle*

THE PAIN NUDGES her awake, boring into her right eye, and in the dark she reaches for the drops, the bottle rocking on the nightstand, and lies back, thinking, *There now. There now.* Thinking that perhaps her mother will have to take the school again, and that will mean another wasted day, long tales about her courtship, her slender ankles. The children will twitch in their chairs, waiting. Waiting until she comes to the part about the storm at sea and the sailor who was washed overboard, the look on his face. *On this day,* Alice thinks, as the warmth moves through her, *on this day there should be no more dwelling on death.*

She slides back into sleep and dreams a memory, as she often has these past long months. The tap on the front door and Mr. Heath on the step, the bright autumn day behind him. She asks if there is a problem with the music Lilian collected and he says no, says that everything is fine. Nothing unusual in his face, nothing in his voice gives any hint. He says that he's sorry to interrupt, that he needs Rachel at home, just for a little while. Down the hall the children's clear voices are chanting: *Seven eights are fifty-six, eight eights are* . . .

She asks him in but Mr. Heath says that he will wait where he is, says something about the clear sky. In the dream her feet are slow and heavy as she moves down the hall to the schoolroom, tells Rachel that her father has come for her, that it's just for a moment, and she can leave her things where they are. The dream Rachel wears a white dress, although in life Alice knows it was a faded blue. She moves down the hall toward the dark shape in the doorway and Alice turns back to the others. Through the schoolroom window she sees them crossing the street, hand in hand.

. . .

Sarah also dreams, dreams a child with blond curls, hugging her around the neck. The chubby arms squeezing tighter and tighter until she is gasping for breath, a long scratch on her neck where she scrabbles to pry them loose. She lies back on the pillow, feeling her pounding heart, and hears the downstairs clock chime. It isn't until she's used the pot, poured water from the pitcher and splashed her face, that she remembers what day it is. She kneels by the side of the bed and gives thanks.

. . .

Alice wakes again with a start, as if at a sudden sound. The back stairs creak and that will be her sister, Sarah, and it will be exactly eight minutes before six. Hours before she needs to be behind her counter at Becks' store, but Alice has never asked why she rises, leaves the house so early. It will be something to do with the cause Mrs. Beck has drawn her in to, leaflets to post or a meeting. She may even go creeping down back lanes, may peer into dawn windows looking for empty bottles, for signs of dissipation. There is nothing wrong, of course not, with wanting to live a pure life. Nothing wrong with the Union, the meetings and speeches. But the thought of her sister standing grim-faced by the tavern door fills Alice with a familiar, helpless fury, and she rolls in her bed and closes her eyes, hoping for just a little more sleep. Finds herself thinking of Mr. Heath, who is surely awake, behind his cell door, tries to imagine what it can possibly be like. Knowing that your life is now measured in hours, in minutes, less time than it takes to ride the train to the city, to read a book from beginning to end. She knows from the newspaper that Reverend Toller will attend the execution, that he has visited a number of times in the months since the trial, and she wonders if his intention was to bring comfort. A man who sat without a flicker of emotion through his own wife's funeral, who turned away when his son began to sob. But what comfort could even a kindlier man bring, what comfort could there be, even in forgiveness, knowing that you wouldn't meet them again in Heaven. That even if you could, they would surely run and hide.

It's more likely, Alice supposes, that Reverend Toller simply kneels and prays, that perhaps they pray together. The same newspaper that called Heath a fiend, a monster, now reports that he spends most of his time sitting silently on the edge of his cot, staring at a spot on the floor. In fact, he has barely spoken since they found him that day, slumped on a cushion of crimson leaves at the base of an oak tree in the heart of Jackson's wood. The gun, with one bullet left, held loosely in his hand.

. . .

Her feet are tangled in her nightdress and the bedclothes are a terrible weight. She kicks them off and feels the cool air on her skin. It is May, late May, and in the time since her first waking the room has appeared, the heavy, dark dressing table, the chair by the window. She closes her eyes again and tests the pain in her head. Still there, but muffled, and the bottle is half full, so maybe it will be all right. The pattern is familiar to her now, although that doesn't make it any easier. Just not as frightening; the first time she thought she must be dying, right there at the dinner table, on her fourteenth birthday. A shimmering in the air as her mother raised the silver knife to cut another slice of cake, the pain suddenly there, where all had been sweet and normal, building and building. As her parents helped her from the room she saw Sarah reach with her fork, spear the crumbling piece left on Alice's plate. Upstairs, it was her father who measured out the liquid from the medicine chest, mixed it with a little sweet red syrup. Alice's stomach heaved when it touched her lips, but there was his cool hand on her forehead, his voice speaking softly, and she held on to that. *Sleep now,* he said, *and all will be well*. And it was.

. . .

Alice's father was a tall man with a trimmed beard, a teller of jokes, an elder of the church, an educated man with a prosperous business. But he died in an upstairs room on Neeve Street, something that was blurted out in those first terrible hours and never referred to again. Their mother took to her bed, the heavy wine-colored drapes pulled tight. Leaving Sarah to talk with the lawyer, to write to the relatives in England, to sit night after night at the kitchen table, her spectacles glinting, working out figures on long sheets of paper. Alice was sixteen then; she'd never given a thought to money, although she knew that the expansion of the shop had meant only one dress that winter and a delay in the new furniture. She sat by the fire through those winter evenings, a book in her lap, the distant scratching of Sarah's pen.

The way they live now is all Sarah's doing, Sarah's plan, but Alice tells herself to be fair, to think about what might have happened, otherwise. It was Sarah's idea to open the school, the real school, to have Alice help, and maybe their mother if she ever opened the drapes. *What else do you have to do?* she said. *What else do you do but sit in your chair by the window, reading poetry all day.*

Sarah organized everything for the school, found a few texts and primers, ordered supplies from the catalog and placed notices, spoke to parents at church. Mrs. Beck came to call and said that although she had no children to send, she would like to donate several Temperance Readers. She said that she was impressed by Sarah's discipline, her organization, that she would like to offer her a position in the store, if Alice and her mother were able to run the school on their own. *Of course we can,* Alice said, although before that moment she wouldn't have thought it. It's clear to her now that otherwise it wouldn't have worked, that Sarah would never have had the patience. At first, parents like the Robinsons sent their children as a kindness, but most have stayed and new ones have come and Alice knows that must mean that she is doing something right. It's been five years and now there's not really enough room around the long oak dining table, sent from England before she was born. Even with the empty place.

· · ·

From downstairs comes the slam of the stove door, the crash of the heavy kettle. Alice thinks of the Orton sisters, who sing so sweetly together, of Lilian and Rachel side by side on their battered porch swing, arms linked. She tries to find one warm memory of her own sister, one time they might have laughed together, been easy in each other's company. *Chalk and cheese* is what their mother used to say, and they couldn't even share a room, let alone a bed, from the time they were small.

When she was a child, Alice thought that her father was a wizard, and his shop was a magic cave, full of potions. Sometimes she sat on the floor in the room behind the counter, lifting the different colored bottles out of their boxes while he pounded and mixed and measured. Sarah sat on a high stool at the corner of his workbench, writing neat labels and spreading them out to dry. *Aconite, Senna, Chloral Hydrate*. When Alice was older she joined her at the bench, but when their father left the room Sarah shook her pen, flinging black drops all over her own careful writing. *I didn't,* she said loudly, *I did not. Alice made the mess, she did.* Their father raised his voice and sent them home, and once outside Alice gave her sister a quick kick in the shins and then ran, Sarah's fingers reaching for her flying hair.

That night their father brought home two large bottles, Alice's blue and Sarah's amber. He had labeled them *Forgiveness Potion* in flowing black letters, and he told them they were to take a spoonful in the morning and at bedtime, until the bottles were empty. The liquid was pale green and sweet, but with something sharper that lingered at the back of the throat. It took weeks to finish, and Alice kept her empty bottle standing up beside her brush and comb. When it disappeared, Sarah said she didn't know anything about it.

· · ·

In the kitchen Sarah stands by the window, waiting for the tea to steep. The peonies Alice planted are covered with tight, round buds and Sarah knows that it's only a matter of time before ants appear inside the house, crawling and sneaking into every space. So like her sister, not thinking of anything beyond the scent through the open window.

Looking past the bushes she sees the Robinsons' back door open, close, but without her glasses everything is a soft blur and she can't tell who comes out. They are not known as early risers. She asked Dr. Robinson to speak at a meeting once, but he shook his head and said he didn't think he'd say what they wanted to hear. When she told Mrs. Beck, she said it was clear there was a great deal of work to do in the town.

There *is* a great deal of work to do, and Sarah can hardly remember what life was like before. The ticking of the clock, the chiming; another hour over. Now there are never enough of them in the day. Leaflets to print and distribute, schemes for raising money, always reports to write and meetings to organize. On her counter at Becks', beside the stylish hats, there is a special wooden rack for their literature, and although it is frequently emptied, the taverns remain open and half the churches still use fermented wine. Her father used to like a glass with dinner, her mother too, and at Christmas he would pour for Sarah and Alice, a mixture that was mostly water. She shudders now to think of it. How those could have been the first steps on the road to ruin. She sees her father's smiling face, thinks of the hours they spent at this kitchen table, going over plans for the shop, adding up columns of figures, and feels nothing but scorn for that foolish girl.

• • •

Alice hears Sarah moving about in her room and knows that she will soon be gone, making her brisk way down the street, the satchel stuffed with pamphlets banging at her leg. She slides her hand under the pillow and it closes around her father's pocket watch, cool against her palm. Sarah had wanted to sell it; she said they needed every cent, that they had to sell everything that had been his, even the shirts and jackets still holding the shape of his arms. She reached into the wardrobe and their mother began to wail, a piercing sound that grew steadily higher, louder. Pulling at Sarah's arm and Sarah shook her off and then somehow their mother was on the floor, rolling back and forth, her hair falling over her face and her skirts all twisted. Howling and batting at the girls when they tried to help her up. They stared at each other, wide-eyed. *Mother,* they said. *Mother.* But she didn't hear. Only calming, slowly, when Sarah said over and over, *I've put them back, I won't touch them again, everything is just as it was. Just as it was.*

Later, in the kitchen, she said, *I can't find his watch; have you seen his watch? She won't notice that, and I could get a good price.* Alice shook her head, and Sarah said then it must have been stolen, it must have been Lucy that stole it. Another reason to let her go.

Alice was never allowed to touch the watch, when she was small and captivated by it, but her father would show her each time she asked. How to press down on the stem to pop open the case, the black hand ticking around, his initials engraved, and a date. His mother gave it to him the night before he sailed, along with a brand-new Bible. One of the grandmothers Alice never met. After she had looked at the face, puzzled out the swirling letters on the case, her father would press another spot to open the back, the tiny wheels and gears moving. He told her it must be kept wound, but she's afraid to wind it now, in case someone hears the ticking.

. . .

When she hears the front door click, Alice swings her feet to the floor. Her head pounds with the movement and she closes her eyes, waiting for it to subside. Remembers her father's cool hand, his voice saying, *It will pass, Alice, and all will be well.* She thinks of all the things she heard her father say, through her life, all the words. And she knows that it is a strange and wonderful thing that from all those days and years of words, these are the only ones that bring with them the sound of his voice. *All will be well, Alice;* she can hear him. *All manner of things will be well.*

If she hurried to the front window she would see Sarah, already a small figure, leaning to the right a little with the weight of her scuffed brown satchel. Instead she goes to her own window, looks down at the grass, so green after all the rain, rolling away to the river where threads of white mist still hover. *Season of mists,* she thinks, but that's another season entirely.

If she went to the front window she would also see the little white house, the *House of Horror,* the newspapers called it. Alice's mother brought home a story the week after the murders. People in town saying there was something evil in the house itself, old Mrs. Hatch saying, in her rustling voice, that she had always known, could have told them, if anyone ever listened. *But many people have lived in that house,* Alice said, *other families.* Her mother stopped, with a hat pin in her hand, said, *And didn't we wonder why they never stayed long?*

Thinking of the house, Alice remembers seeing them all on the front porch, Mrs. Heath and the girls standing back while Mr. Heath turned the key, ushered them inside with a little bow, a flourish of his hand. *That will be Mr. Marl's new bookkeeper,* her mother had said, standing at the window beside her. *They don't have many things, do they?*

Some days later she and Sarah called with their mother, carrying a plate of cakes, roses from their garden. Mrs. Heath, Naomi, asked first about the church, about who her husband should talk to about a pew. She said that they had come from Toronto, that things had been very difficult there. That Mr. Marl's advertisement had appeared like an answer to a prayer. She was pleased to hear about the Barnes' school, just across the way, said that her older daughter stayed at home, but she would speak to her husband about Rachel attending. The two girls carried in a tray of tea things and then took their places on the settee on either side of their mother, although there wasn't really room.

· · ·

Sarah walks the long way around so she can stop by the railway station before she goes to the store. The world is clearer with her glasses and there are more people about than she's used to this early, hooves and creaking cart wheels and the sound of voices. They are all moving toward the jail, even though there will be nothing to see, the execution taking place behind its high walls. She wonders if Heath can hear the voices, alone in his cell, if he hears the tone, the way his name is spoken. She hopes he does, hope it makes him quake; she still can't believe how completely she was fooled. Those times he helped her with the Sunday school, the plans they made for excursions and concerts, for lessons. Not a hint of his black, black heart.

The heavy door of the station creaks as she pushes it open. The lamps are still burning and the room is empty, except for Abel Timms at his counter, the scratch of his pen as he writes in a big brown book. He nods to Sarah but then looks down again; she's seen him staggering out of Malley's tavern more than once. As usual, someone has emptied the rack and the papers lie strewn about the floor, some crumpled, some marked with muddy bootprints. She returns those that are not badly soiled, and adds a few new ones from her satchel. *TREMBLE, KING ALCOHOL!,* one says. And, *WHAT ABOUT THE CHILDREN?*

Sarah's father always said she had a fine mind, a man's mind, said she would go to the new university when the shop improvements were paid for. She can't help thinking about the different way she would have known this station. Waiting for the early morning train, coming back on Friday nights with her head stuffed full of everything she'd learned. She would have shared rooms in the city, would have met girls who were more like her, who talked about things besides the latest styles and who was walking out together. But she reminds herself that if things hadn't changed she wouldn't have come to know Mrs. Beck in the same way; she would have been exposed to all kinds of dangers without the clear knowledge she now possesses, without any kind of weapon against them. She would have married her fiancé, Gordon, and he might have become a drunkard, making her life a misery. The first time she stood on a platform her legs were trembling so much she didn't think she could do it, but she did do it, and the audience applauded, and the women welcomed her like a member of a family.

•   •   •

In the kitchen there's a sprinkling of crumbs on the table, a puddle of tea that Alice suspects has been deliberately poured, splashing the cover of the book that she doesn't remember leaving just there. The pain nags behind her eye while she prepares her mother's tray, reminding her that it is covered up, but not gone. She toasts bread and cooks an egg in its shell, pours a cup of tea and adds the last of the milk, two spoons of sugar. She takes a bite from a crust of bread but spits it out again. When her father was alive they ate breakfast together in the dining room, and they still had Lucy to prepare it and bring the plates to the table. Alice's mother wore her pink wrap, but her hair was brushed and pinned up and she told them all what she planned to do that day. Three afternoons a week she taught needlework and comportment to six young women whose mothers worried about their chances. When the weather was fine, they often took little stools out the back and sketched the trees and the flowers. Up in her own room, working on her lessons, Alice could smell lilacs through the open window, hear their voices twittering, swooping.

Lucy works for the Robinsons now, and a girl from across the river comes twice a week to do the heavy work and some of the laundry. They tried to manage on their own the first year, another of Sarah's economies, but even she admitted it was too much. The cooking, the cleaning, the washing, the mending. Carpets not beaten for months on end, the stove not blackened. They talked about a Home Girl, but remembered one they had tried years before. Worse than useless, their mother said; she had to be shown every little thing, and woke them with her crying in the night. Mr. Heath told her once that the ship they came out on was filled with Home Children; very hard on his wife, he said, though he didn't say why.

Life is easier now. Not like before, but not such a struggle, and there's even time for a walk, some days, time to turn the pages of a book. Although for Sarah it's only the Bible now, and she reads in a hard-backed chair at the kitchen table. Papers spread out, working on her lectures, her leaflets. Sometimes, walking through the room, Alice expects to see her father there; it reminds her so much of those months of planning the expansion of the shop, working out how much could be raised or borrowed. That Christmas it was almost ready, the shelves built and the walls painted, a new, bigger sign over the door.

After the burial their mother took to her bed with the drapes drawn and when she did get up, days later, Alice had to help her decide what dress to put on. She's better now; she walks to the grocer, the butcher; she prepares the meals and on their birthdays makes her special honey cake. But she seems to list a little when she walks, and the smallest thing will have her in a fluster. She likes to help in the school but her mind doesn't stay on the lesson, and before long she is talking about a ballroom glowing with hundreds of candles, the line of young men with their hands held out to her. The children don't mind. They put down their pencils and listen, or pretend to listen, to stories they've heard time and again. The slyer ones knowing the questions to ask, how to take them all farther and farther away from the open arithmetic text. The children don't mind, but Alice does; she's become quite serious about the school. Even the first fumbling year she realized that it was something she liked, and more, something she was good at. Finding the key to each child, seeing their brows unfurrow. She thinks, although she hasn't mentioned it yet, that she would like to go for her certificate if the money can be found. And then maybe teach in the new high school and who knows, maybe some of her pupils will go on to do great things. Maybe one of them will say, years later, *I owe it all to my teacher, my first real teacher.*

. . .

Upstairs, Alice sets down the tray and goes into her own room, takes one swig from the bottle before she carries on down the hall, opens her mother's door. As she pulls at the heavy drapes she thinks that they really should be cleaned. The girl might do it, but she'd have to be paid extra and Sarah would have something to say about that.

It's a quarter past seven, she says, and her mother groans and reaches to touch the silver framed photograph beside the bed. Alice's father adored her mother; no one told her that, but it was something she always knew. Maybe the way he bent his head to hear her light voice, the way he loved to tease. Once her mother stood before him, in a shimmering new dress made up by Miss Bolt. *Oh, my dear,* he said, sternly. *That color . . .* Putting aside his newspaper, walking slowly around her, taking a bit of fabric between his fingers. Stroking his chin. *It's really too . . . too perfect,* he said, and Sarah and Alice laughed and laughed at the look on their mother's face; she swatted at him and said, *Oh, Andrew,* and he laughed too, all of them laughing together. And Alice was struck by something that she'd never thought of before, by the fact that her parents were *people,* that they had lives before her, and without her. She was so taken with this thought that she whispered it to Sarah, who squinted her eyes behind her new spectacles and said, *What are you talking about? How silly you are; of course they're people. What else did you think they were?* Later, in her room, Alice took a piece of paper and wrote her thought down. She's certain she slipped it between the pages of a book, but she no longer remembers what book it was. Wonders if she will come across it years from now, and what it will be like, to see her childish hand again. Wonders if there will be anyone she can show it to. Once she had known, just known, that she would marry a handsome, brooding man who would somehow cross her path. Nothing like Sarah's Gordon, with his heavy eyebrows, his awkward hands. Nothing like the boyish boys her friends whispered about. Not long before that terrible Christmas her family sat for the photographer, and with his wild hair, his slender, stained fingers, with the way his words spun and flowed, Alice could hardly breathe when he touched her cheek, when he moved her head, just a little.

She met him again by chance, the first time by chance, walking by the river with a small book in her hand. He was setting up his camera on its heavy tripod and he asked if she would read to him while he worked; her voice sounded thin and a little silly at first, but soon she was lost in the words. He told her that an idea had just come to him, that he would photograph the same view every few days, the river, seen through one curving branch, that he would do it until the branch was completely bare. That first day the afternoon sun was still warm, the leaves just slightly tinged with orange.

She never saw the photographer in town, even when she strolled past his studio, but he always seemed happy to meet her when he came to the place by the river, and sometimes she read, but mostly she listened to his talk. He let her look through to the view he was framing, let her see what he saw, and once he stroked her neck with the back of his hand. She cringes to think of it now, how obvious her infatuation must have been, although at the time she felt so grown up. He asked her once how old she was, laughed and said he'd have to wait for her, and she wrapped the idea around herself like the woolen shawl she wore to the riverbank when the branch was bare, thinking that he might still appear.

. . .

She could go another way, but Sarah doesn't believe in giving in, and so she makes herself walk down Norfolk Street. And there is the shop, Mr. Marl's shop now. He is not a pharmacist, of course; someone else actually runs it. But it is his name above the door, gilt letters on a deep blue ground. He gave them a fair price, though not the fairest. True, there were debts to pay, but Sarah's father had planned it well and all Mr. Marl had to do was repaint the sign, turn the key in the door, and start making money. She can't stop the thought that says how proud her father would be at the shop's success. It was a part of her life for as long as she can remember, her father teaching her the names of things, the properties, introducing her to each customer. *This is my daughter Sarah.* Resting his hand on her head.

Later Alice started coming and spoiled it all, but Sarah waited her out. She had always been good with figures, was already helping with the books and checking the stock, learning to mix the simpler preparations. While Alice lived her child's life, giggling with her friends and mooning over words, just words. No help at all the winter it all ended, sobs from behind her bedroom door, from behind their mother's. What did they think—that they would survive by magic?

Sarah didn't cry, not then, not later. Only once. Sitting with Mr. Heath in the Sunday school, after the children had gone. They had let the stove go out and the room grew quickly cold while they talked about arranging a party for Easter, about the problem of Robert Bride, who memorized a hundred verses every week and always took home the certificate. And then somehow they were talking about Sarah's mother, and how she couldn't even decide what vegetable to cook for their dinner. About the way her father went out that winter night, saying he needed a little air. *There there,* William said, patting her shoulder. *There there.* Soon he will burn in Hell, and though she knows it's wrong, she is glad.

· · ·

Alice coils her hair, looking into the spotted mirror. She touches the high collar, buttoned at her neck. There are things she should be doing but the laudanum has made her movements slower, and nothing at all seems urgent. She knows the children will be edgy when they come, unsettled, for they all know what day it is; everyone in Emden knows what day it is. She had thought of making some special cakes, something to distract them, but realized that would seem like a celebration. She holds the banister when she makes her way downstairs, her feet seeming a little distant, not quite part of her body. In the schoolroom she opens the shutters and sunlight reaches for the long table, the chairs, the map tacked up on the wall. Rachel's father came for her on a day filled with blue sky, said it was just for a moment, and she left her copybook open, her new pencil lying on top. It was the first thing Alice saw when she opened the door the next morning.

Rachel's things are now in a tidy pile in Alice's room; there is no one left to return them to. Page after page of problems copied out and solved, compositions and the carefully drawn maps with their secret signs for mountains and lakes and forests. A folder of pictures she had drawn, several of her family standing all together in front of their little white house. She wasn't best at drawing people but she did the house very well, taking great care with the swing on the front porch, the fanlight over the door. Through the front windows, one up, two down, she sketched hazy shapes in one of the pictures, a glimpse of what was inside. Try as she might, Alice can't make out what the shapes are supposed to be.

Although she took away the books and papers, she couldn't bring herself to touch Rachel's chair, but Alice began to see that it was not the best thing to have it there, so solidly empty, when the children took their places around the table. She noticed how careful they were not to touch it as they went by, and one Saturday she moved it up to her bedroom too, placed the other things neatly on it. But still no one fills that space at the table.

Rachel was the easiest child; sunny-natured, curious and quick to learn. In the first days after the murders, Alice was appalled to find herself thinking that there were others it would not have been so tragic to lose. She didn't know the family well, didn't really know them at all. Words exchanged on the church steps, in the street. They seemed a solemn group, Mr. Heath's stern face and his wife in her layers of black, Lilian's small voice and downcast eyes. But knowing Rachel as she did, what she was like, Alice had to believe that it had been a contented home, maybe a happy one.

It was difficult for a time after, the children inattentive and skittish, and Alice herself unsure of the best way to proceed. They had all known death, in their families or among friends and neighbors, but nothing like this and it clutched at her heart as she looked at their faces, noticed the dark smudges under Eaton's eyes, and thought that they were right to be afraid. She knew that it would be callous to expect them to carry on with their lessons as if nothing had changed and that first day she led them out the door, through the leaf-littered streets, and they spent the afternoon walking in the wood at the edge of town, where maple keys spiraled down all around them. The children found their voices in the wood, and once Lucius ran ahead, jumped out from behind a thick trunk and made the girls shriek. Alice had them gather up all the different leaves they could find, and brittle keys and acorns, and she asked them if they knew that Emden, with its streets and stone buildings, the houses where they lived, had once been forest just like this, and not so very long ago. Nina said she thought it would be nicer if the trees had stayed and they could all live in them, and for once no one laughed at her. Bella asked why every acorn didn't make a tree and Alice told her that she didn't really know, only that from the hundreds that fell in the wood only some would take root and grow, and sometimes it took years to even begin.

Then Eaton asked how old the maple tree was. *This one,* he said, slapping it with his hand. *Very old,* Alice said, looking up at the thick, spreading branches. *But how old?* Eaton said, and there was a roughness in his voice that she hadn't ever heard. *How would you know how old it is?* Eaton said, and Alice told him, told them all, that when a tree was cut down rings were visible in the stump, that you could count the rings and know the age of the tree. *But then it's dead,* Eaton said, and she could tell that he'd already known about the rings, that for some reason he'd wanted to hear her say it. *If you cut it down it's dead,* Eaton said, *so how can it even matter?*

·   ·   ·

Reporters from the city paper had come knocking, as they were sitting down to their evening meal. Alice's mother led them in to the front room, and the one with the lazy eye prowled around, picking up ornaments as if he were in a shop or in his own house; he even crossed the hall and poked his head into the darkened schoolroom. *Our readers like the details,* he said as he sat down again, his good eye meeting Alice's. Making notes in his little book while the one with the mustard-colored jacket went on with his questions. *You heard nothing at all? No screams? No shots?* he said. *Nothing,* Alice said. Her mother dabbed at her eyes with her lace-edged handkerchief, murmuring, *Poor things, poor things.*

Mr. Luft from the *Herald* had asked the same questions, and before him Constable Street, when he came to tell Alice to send the children away early. He had been the one, the night her father didn't come home. Calling for Sarah and Alice, calling for water, after their mother swooned. When they came running they found him cradling her head in his big red hands.

Like Mr. Luft, these reporters also asked about money. Said they'd heard about some dishonesty, an embezzlement charge, but all Alice could tell them was that the school fees were paid on time, that the family lived simply, but was far from the poorest in town. The questions went on and on, until her mother spoke up, loudly. *They were a fine family,* she said. *A good, Christian family. There was nothing different about them, nothing peculiar.*

Listening to her mother, Alice thought how true it was. They sat two pews in front in church and she knew the back of their heads, Mr. Heath's thick brown hair neatly cut, Naomi's untrimmed black bonnet. Lilian's thin shoulders and the strange little noises she sometimes made. She thought of the words she'd exchanged with each of them, of the words she'd heard them say to each other. If there had been some clue, some hint, she had missed it completely and so, it seemed, had everyone else.

. . .

Lazy Eye turned a page in his notebook, the pencil held tight in his fat fingers. Alice wondered what kind of story he would write, when so little seemed to be known. When her father died, the *Herald* said only that it had been sudden, and a terrible loss to the town. Christmas Day, and she remembered the cold air, snow squeaking beneath their feet as they walked from church, the dazzling reflection of the sun. The new curate had a problem with his speech, and her father mimicked him all the way home. *I'm sho hungry*, he said. *I wonder wash for luncheon thish day. Stop,* their mother said, her mouth twitching a smile. *Stop,* she said, taking her hand from her muff and slapping at his arm. *Someone will hear you.*

Shtop? he said. *Did you shay you want me to shtop?* Waving a hand as Mr. Marl drove by, the horses' harnesses jingling. As they stamped off the snow outside their door her father said in a loud whisper, *The wagesh of shin ish*—and they were all giggling as they stepped inside, the smell of cloves all through the house. Nothing unusual in the rest of that day, meals prepared and small gifts opened, their mother lighting the lamps as the night drew in while Sarah played from the sheet music Gordon had given her, tied with white ribbon and a clumsy bow. Their father saying, when she was finished, that he thought he'd take a little stroll, that he thought he'd get some air. Bending to kiss their mother's cheek, and the way she tilted her face to receive that kiss, and looked back down at her book. Alice would have said that she knew her father, would never have thought to question that. But as he bent to kiss her mother, as he wrapped the gray scarf around his neck and stepped out into the cold, clear night, his mind must have been on the perfumed rooms on Neeve Street, no sign of that on his familiar face.

Yellow Jacket crossed one sharp knee over the other and asked why they thought such a thing would happen, if they had any ideas at all. *Drink,* Sarah said, *that will be at the bottom of it,* and both reporters leaned forward in their chairs, but when she admitted that she'd never actually seen Mr. Heath take a drop, they sat back again. Then Lazy Eye stood, cutting off her lecture, and said that they had to be going. In the kitchen, Alice scraped their cold supper into the pail.

. . .

Sarah holds her coat closed at the neck; she's been cold for years, it seems, wears extra layers on all but the hottest days of summer. She remembers that she once saw the murdered girl and the Robinson boy sitting on the grass at the river's edge, wriggling their bare toes in the sun. For some reason it had made her think of the back room in the pharmacy, the smell of spices and earth and medicines, the way the light there seemed to make everything glow.

Mrs. Beck is the only one Sarah can depend on now. The one who has helped her find her way. Things she used to worry about, listening to Reverend Toller's sermons—Mrs. Beck has shown her that those things are really her strengths, what make her such a valuable worker for the cause. Sometimes, before she falls asleep, she imagines herself saving Mrs. Beck from a fire, pushing her out of the way of a runaway horse and wagon. Often Sarah is badly hurt; sometimes she dies. She hears Mrs. Beck weeping, hears her say, as she has heard her say in life, *She's the daughter I never had.*

It was Mrs. Beck who showed her that what happened with Gordon was a good thing, the broken engagement all for the best. There were a few tears, but Mrs. Beck dried Sarah's eyes with her own handkerchief, explained how it was clear that Gordon didn't really support their work, would maybe have forbidden it. *It will take time,* she said, *but you will be so glad.*

Mrs. Beck is always early at the store; she likes to be there herself to let little Donal in with his broom, to give him a bit of bread and jam for his breakfast. Through Donal she hopes to reach the entire family, and there are already signs that this is happening, tears in the mother's eyes as she tried to sit up in her fusty bed. From the very beginning Mrs. Beck told Sarah that they must be vigilant, that opportunities are everywhere, not just in the meeting hall, and they must seize them.

While Donal sweeps, Mrs. Beck and Sarah check both floors of the store, making sure that everything is neatly piled, the correct things in the correct drawers. From the first, Mrs. Beck was pleased with Sarah's sharp eye. Mr. Beck arrives later, in time to lead the morning prayers. His heart is not strong and he does less and less, but he likes to sit at his desk looking over things; he likes to get up and greet good customers by name, ask after their families. Sarah went to him when she saw Reverend Toller's wife slip the buttons into her pocket, and two days later a pair of soft kid gloves, and he dealt with it discreetly, called on her husband, who thanked him for his consideration. When Mrs. Toller died last summer, Mrs. Beck was not the only one who whispered about blessings in disguise.

This morning, most of the other clerks are a little late stepping through the back door; they have stopped outside the jail and there is a hum beneath their voices when they say good morning to Mr. Beck, good morning to Mrs. Beck and Sarah. It is already a quarter to eight. Mr. Beck opens the prayer book and they all bow their heads as he begins to read: *O Lord, we beseech thee, absolve thy people from their offenses; that through thy bountiful goodness we may all be delivered from the bands of those sins, which by our frailty we have committed.* He has a surprisingly deep voice, a rolling voice that always reminds Sarah of the way her father used to read aloud in the evenings. Staring down at her clasped hands she is swept by a sudden wave of longing for the warm sound of her father's voice, a pool of yellow light. She bites at her trembling lower lip, as hard as she can. Words she has heard, words she has read in the hard-backed kitchen chair, surge through her mind, and though she tries to concentrate on her clasped hands, on the gouge in the floorboards at her feet, the words keep coming. *For thou, Lord, art good, and ready to forgive. Look upon mine affliction and my pain.*

There is a murmured *Amen,* and Mr. Beck closes his book; the little group separates as he makes his way to open the front door. Sarah walks toward her counter and maybe someone speaks to her, but her head is filled with words, just words, going around and around. *And I will take away the stony heart out of your flesh, and I will give you an heart of flesh.* She touches the soft plume on a trim brown hat, straightens the pamphlets in the rack once more. She is suddenly so tired, thinks of the long day ahead, the errands to do at noontime, the meeting this evening which is sure to run late. She would like to close her eyes, thinks that if she could rest, just a little bit, it would be enough. *Our life is but a sleep and a forgetting,* she thinks, more words pushing around in her mind, but she knows they're not quite right. Alice would know; Alice can recite all kinds of verses, with a contented, dreamy look on her face. Though she knows that she won't do it, Sarah thinks of telling Mrs. Beck that she is ill, thinks of going home again, of walking quickly home. And Alice will tell her the words and she will climb the stairs with an easy mind, lie down and sleep clean through the day.

. . .

By ten minutes to eight Alice is ready, hears a sigh and a shuffle from her mother's room and knows that she is at least on her feet. She pours another few spoonsful from the bedside bottle; it is almost empty and she wonders if she will have time, when the children go for their lunch, to go to Howell's for another. Mr. Marl's is closer, but she doesn't shop there. It sometimes lasts for days, this pain; it wears her down. Her mother tries to make her take to her bed, her cure for everything, but Alice remembers what her father used to say, that it's always better to fight than to give in. All the stories he used to tell about coming to this country to make a new life, the hardships and the satisfactions. She thinks that if he were still alive they would be part of something larger, that without him they are all just fumbling through, even Sarah, who seems so sure.

She sits in the blue chair by her bedroom window and wonders what is happening now, imagines the clank of a metal door opening, the sound of heavy feet. *Ye know neither the day nor hour,* she thinks, and wonders again what it must be like if you *do* know. When Rachel first started coming to the school she asked about Alice's father, and when Alice said he was dead she said, *You must be so sad. I don't know how I could bear it if something happened to my papa.*

What a good thing she won't know, Alice thinks, and then she remembers.

People said all kinds of things after the arrest, and later when the trial stirred it all up again. People who didn't know him at all claimed to have heard Mr. Heath muttering to himself, looking at them with murderous eyes. The newspapers reported every detail, told how his lawyer tried to argue that he was insane. It was obvious, the lawyer said, that a man would have to be insane to do what he did. Alice understood the argument, of course she did, and yet . . . He stood on her front step that blue autumn day, his plan already half carried out, nothing in his voice, nothing in his expression, and Alice knows it was not so simple. Knows that he had reasons, some kind of reasons, that it was the only way he saw. Knows that if he had spoken at all, these past long months, he would have said it was done out of love.

According to the newspaper the execution apparatus is of a new design, and will perform its function quickly and painlessly. There are many who say that is not how it should be. A diagram had been drawn beside the article, smudgy lines that could have been a picture of anything. Alice has never been behind the high walls of the jail, although Sarah goes regularly to pass out her literature. She could have asked Sarah what it was like, and then she would have been able to picture it, but she rarely talks to Sarah, except about the details of the household. She only knew about Gordon because his sister told her after church one day that he had broken off the engagement. *He says she's changed,* Beth whispered, bending her head close so no one could overhear. *All this preaching and standing outside taverns, handing things out on the street. He says he just couldn't go on with it.*

At home Alice said that she'd heard, said she was sorry, and Sarah batted a hand in the air. *Who would take the three of us on?* she said, turning away, as if that were the reason. *I don't care at all,* Sarah said, and Alice chose to believe her. She thinks now of the red lines where Sarah's spectacles sit, of the way she rubs at her eyes when she takes them off. She thinks of her sister's narrow shoulders in her old black coat, and the way the satchel bumps at her leg, the way she seems coiled tight, like a watch that is wound and wound.

Rachel's chair stands, wedged in the corner, the little pile of books and papers. Downstairs the clock chimes for eight o'clock, and on the second note the church bell begins to toll, and she knows that it is done. She thinks that perhaps she will take the children back to the wood, where things are now green and growing. She has time to decide, and she has the whole day to think of what she will say, when Sarah opens the door.

HOUSE

THE HOUSE IS still empty but already people walk by it without stopping, without a shudder in the mind. Sometimes they arrive at their destination and realize that. It's a small white house with a long front porch, one window up, two down, on either side of the door that has always been firmly shut. The floor plan was reproduced in the newspaper, neat crosses where the bodies were found, so although few people were ever inside, anyone can imagine. Perhaps in another year or so someone else will move in, someone too stolid or too poor to mind; the rent will stay low for years to come.

Mr. Marl owns the white house; he pays a man to keep the yard tidy, to rake up the twigs and dead grass, burn the fallen leaves. Boards have been nailed over the shattered windows, but other than that it looks like any other house, no sign at all. There was some bad feeling against him, talk that his son-in-law passed on, claiming concern. The glint in Lett's eyes reminding

Marl of things that would have to be dealt with, when this other business was done. There was muttering on street corners and even a suggestion in the newspaper, when the fact of the embezzlement charge became known, the arrest. As if he was somehow to blame, as if he had caused it all. Marl had a moment of doubt, eyes wide open in his soft bed, but only a moment; he knew that it was nonsense, nothing to do with him. He was, in fact, another victim, his trust betrayed, but no one seemed to care about that. When Heath had first presented himself, Marl already knew that his circumstances were desperate. He saw the brushed lapels, the battered boots that were newly cleaned and polished. Noted the way Heath carried himself, the way he spoke, carefully, but without even a hint of pleading. He recognized him as a proud man who wanted something better, a man who only needed a chance, and would be grateful for it. He saw something of his own younger self; maybe that was his mistake.

Although it belonged to him, Mr. Marl had the furniture sold along with the family's few possessions, and added the amount to the fund he used for expenses. The funerals, the small, flat stones, the inquiry agents in England. The lawyer from the city, who had to be paid by someone. The sale raised more than he had expected but a significant amount still had to come from his own pocket, and there was also the upkeep of the house, and the stolen amount, never traced, never recovered. Lying in his soft bed he thought how unfair it was, the things people whispered; it was never about the money.

CONSEQUENCES

What will not a fearful man conceive in the dark?

—*The Anatomy of Melancholy*

FOR A LITTLE while that night, maybe even for a long while, he was gloriously drunk. The whiskey sipped before the meal, the wine, the brandy glass that was filled again and again at the round table in Blyth's private dining room. The men sitting with him all fine fellows, the stories they told making him laugh until tears ran down his cheeks. It seemed a lifetime ago that the sheriff had poured a slug of rum, the neck of the bottle rattling against the thick rim of the glass. Rattling and rattling. *I've seen some things,* the sheriff had said. No need to finish the sentence. A second slug after the formality of the inquest, something that had to be done, though they all knew very well how he had died.

Heath's face showed nothing of his last long minutes, looking—not peaceful, but empty. Blank as a photograph, an arrangement of eyes, nose, mouth. The full graying beard that could have belonged to anyone, except for the terrible marks of the rope that were visible beneath it. There was a piece of paper wrapped around the middle finger of the left hand, held tightly by an India rubber band. Robinson took it off, unrolled it, and saw that it was a note written in a child's careful hand, a red heart in each corner. He showed it to the others and then wrapped it back around the limp finger, trying to match the creases the rubber band had made.

The sheriff let them out through a small door in the farthest corner of the yard. *He needed the money,* he said, meaning the red-haired hangman who had bolted at the first sign that things had gone wrong. There would be trouble over that, Robinson not the only one who recognized him as a cousin of the sheriff's wife, recently arrived from Glasgow. Certain not to have been paid the whole amount the sheriff had been given to travel to the city and hire an experienced man. Maybe this time it would be trouble the sheriff couldn't wriggle out of, although from the look of the cousin's flying heels he wouldn't stop running until he was miles from any questions.

As he made his way home, avoiding the crowd still gathered in front of the jail, Robinson remembered looking up as the procession made its way to the dangling rope, and again as they filed back across the yard, their witnessing over. Above the high wall he saw men on the rooftops of buildings across the way, and even faces peering down through the branches of trees. He walked quickly now, keeping his head down, noticing each small sensation. The sweat beginning to gather beneath his collar, the tickle in his nose that meant he was about to sneeze, the small stone lodged inside his left shoe. Things it seemed he still had a right to feel, and Heath did not.

· · ·

There was a bottle in the bottom drawer of his desk, and he noticed that his hand was quite steady as he poured. Leaning back in his chair, feeling the warmth in his throat, in his gut, he thought of them all, but mostly of Lilian. Her bony shoulders, wrists, her voice like the whisper of a turning page. If they'd had more time he knew he could have cured her, and he thought about what that would have meant, for both of them. Even without the note he would have sent to the *Medical Record*, maybe the *Lancet*. Had there been something he should have seen, when Heath came to settle the bill? But that was days before, the awful thought surely not yet a flicker. He knew that even the token he charged could be a hardship, said there was no hurry, none at all, but Heath insisted, removing the coins from a little pouch in his pocket. Try as he might, Robinson couldn't remember anything else they might have said to each other.

He had never warmed to Heath, and sipping slowly now, he wondered about that. They hadn't spoken before the day that Lilian collapsed in a peal of church bells, but he had seen him about in the town, seen the family out walking, knew that the younger girl was at the Barnes' school with his son. People said that Heath had always put on airs, but Robinson didn't think it was exactly that, and he could think of many others who didn't have a penny to pinch, yet carried themselves with dignity and weren't judged for it. There was something in his manner though, something in the way he spoke when he refused the treatment Robinson suggested, denied that Lilian had any need of it. His wife put a hand on his arm, turned her beautiful pale face toward him, and Robinson had seen enough married couples not to be surprised when she returned alone the next day and said that her husband had changed his mind.

Rubbing his eyes with the heels of his hands, the bottle firmly back in the drawer, he wished he had thought to drink a toast to the dead girls. To all the dead girls. In the early years of their marriage, Marianne had conceived again and again, but those possibilities fell away like petals. One did come to term but was born waxy and still, a light fuzz of hair on her delicate skull. They named her Eleanor and sometimes he thought she'd stayed and grown; sometimes he thought he heard her voice from another room.

· · ·

There was no need but he walked the path to the stable anyway, and found the food bin empty, Prince snickering and nudging at his shoulder. It was Eaton's job to see to the horse before he went to school, unlike him to forget. Marianne had been complaining, but then she often did. The tears in Eaton's jacket, the mud on the knees of his trousers, wrinkling her nose when he came into a room and sending him to wash. *He's a boy,* Robinson said, *stop fussing.* But neglecting responsibilities was a different matter. The murders had happened months before, Eaton's screaming nightmares now coming only rarely, but that didn't mean that everything was as it had been. At the funeral Robinson sat next to the aisle and when the boys walked past, carrying the small white coffin, he saw his son like a stranger, jaw clenched and something stony in his face. He meant to talk to Eaton that night, to sit down in the office maybe, just the two of them, but he was called out to a difficult birth. Tiptoed up the stairs just before dawn, still holding the image of a wisp of hair stirred by the sleeping baby's breath. It seemed just a heartbeat before that Eaton had been a tiny wrapped bundle, held tight in Marianne's arms. Robinson in the doorway, feeling the twin skewers of joy and shame.

. . .

The grain rattled in the bin, the metal handle of the water bucket cut into his palm; there was a warm smell of horse, of clean straw, and he remembered standing just like this on a winter afternoon, some years before. Remembered sudden shouting and how he dropped the same bucket, came into the house just as the front door crashed inward, a wild-eyed man he recognized but couldn't at first name, breathing hard. In his arms a boy, legs hanging down, hair stiff with ice. *The river,* the man said. Timms, his name was, Abel Timms. *He went through,* Timms said.

In the kitchen the stove was burning hot and they swept aside the silver Lucy was polishing; it fell clanging to the floor as they laid the boy on the table. It was clear he'd been in the water some time, his face bluish, his skin so cold, but Robinson sent Lucy for blankets, unbuttoned the jacket, the shirt. Rolled him over and thumped his back between the narrow shoulder blades. Lucy shooed the cluster of people out of the doorway and together they took off the boots, cutting the laces, took off the heavy trousers and wrapped him in the blankets until only the small face showed. Timms stood back against the wall, his hands clenched in his hair.

There was nothing to be done but Robinson did it anyway, rubbing the hands, the stick-thin arms, raising the eyelids with his fingers, rolling the body over and back again. A trickle of water from the freckled nose seemed like a miracle until he realized that it was only ice, melting. There were welts on the boy's face, a bump over one eye, and a faraway part of him noticed that, but let it be. *He's gone, Abel,* he finally said, and Timms slid down to the floor, knees up, face buried in his hands. For what seemed like a long time the only sound was the drip of water from the edge of the table.

Lying awake that night Robinson thought about the boy, whose name he still hadn't heard. Thought of him lying on another kitchen table while shadowy women cleaned him with soft cloths, patted him dry. By now he'd be dressed in the best clothes he had, hands folded, marks of the comb in his hair. Lying in a box with one lamp burning and someone keeping watch, as if he could still feel loneliness. Robinson had thought there was nothing left to touch him, had thought his heart was stone. But everything inside him had screamed when the door smashed open, the boy the size of his own son, the sodden jacket so very similar. When he lifted the small, cold flap, Eaton's blue eye looked back at him.

· · ·

He knew Marianne's dilemma, could almost see the thoughts chasing round in her head as they faced each other across the table, knives in their hands. How much she wanted to know, wrestling with how she hated to need anything from him, even news. There were times he played with that, but just then he didn't have the heart for it. He told her how it had been and she said, *Good.* Said, *He should have suffered.* It was what the whole town had been saying, what Robinson himself might have felt, if he hadn't seen it.

Marianne's fork moved steadily from her plate to her mouth, the flesh at her neck folding around the high collar of her dress. He asked about Eaton and she said that he had been rude, had rushed right past her and up the stairs, saying something about a headache. Robinson thought of the untended horse, said he would look in on the boy, said he would speak to him. She looked up at him and he suddenly knew that there was something she could say, some word, or even just the tone of her voice saying it; he knew that if she said the right thing, it would make a difference. Instead she reached for the absurd little bell by her glass, asked Lucy to bring more potatoes for the Doctor, and the moment was gone. She spoke again but it no longer mattered and he looked at the silver-handled bell, the same one that had sat on the fine linen cloth by her mother's right hand, the same tinkling notes that had seemed, all those years ago, like the sound of everything he had ever wanted.

He heard Eaton's name, and knew what she would be saying. At one time she had held their son so tightly, crooned to him as he lay in her arms, but from the moment he put on trousers it seemed he brought nothing but trouble. The noise he made and the mess, even though he was, compared to most, a quiet boy. Not his fault that he grew out of his clothes almost as soon as he put them on, surely not surprising that he sometimes dropped things, broke things, tracked mud into the house. Left mud on the floors that Marianne, after all, did not have to clean. Sometimes he saw a look on his son's face, a baffled, helpless look. It seemed to Robinson that she wanted Eaton to be the boy who sat between them in the family photograph they'd had taken. The boy with the unstained jacket, with all his shirt buttons, the boy who sat with his hair neatly combed and didn't move, didn't say a word. And there was sometimes the unwelcome, flickering thought that Eaton would be punished all his life in place of Robinson himself. He thought again that he should talk to his son, maybe take him along on his country visits one day, the way

he used to before the diphtheria scare. There would be time
to explain some things about mothers, about men and women.
Time to tell him that he would grow up and it wouldn't matter,
that none of it was his fault.

. . .

Marianne had stopped talking and he couldn't bear to watch her
chewing mouth. It was just past noon, the sun at its highest
point, but the dining room was in shady light and looking past
her he saw the gently shifting new leaves on the maple tree outside the window. He was suddenly weary, just terribly weary,
and he wondered how they had arrived at this place. It had happened slowly, he knew it must have happened slowly, but it
seemed that he had closed his eyes for a moment, opened them
again and found that they were here, separated by the polished
table in the middle of a long day, without a kind thought in their
heads.

There was a time when he knew everything. Moved with a
jaunty step along city streets, knowing he was being noticed in
his well-cut suit. Top of his class at the School of Medicine, en-
gaged to a girl with round blue eyes, the softest cheek. All that
he had left behind quite firmly sealed away, his life rolling out
ahead of him, bathed in golden light. There were things he
might have thought about, but he didn't. Marianne had pouted,
in her pretty way, when he told her that he wouldn't be able
to take her to the concert, that the invitation to the Professor's
house was not something to be turned down. Perhaps he should
have paid more attention to the way her expression changed
so easily, how it was weeks before she allowed him to kiss her
again. But he was so young then, so sure, and Marianne's eyes
were the clearest blue. He didn't even think of her when he and

Smith inspected each other on the doorstep, flicking bits of dust from the ends of their trousers, the toes of their shoes. The Professor's invitations were rare, and they both knew it meant something. The maid who opened the door stood aside for them, and in the light of the entrance hall the rich carpet seemed to glow, leading them forward. *Yes,* Robinson said to himself. *Oh, yes.*

. . .

He waited until Marianne had made her way up to rest, pulling on the banister, before he climbed the stairs himself and quietly opened the door to Eaton's room. His son lay on his side, facing the tall window, the bedclothes pulled up so that only the top of his ear, a tousle of brown hair showed. Robinson said his name, stepped forward so that he could see more of his face, but Eaton seemed to be sound asleep and he left the room as carefully as he had entered it. Downstairs in the kitchen Lucy dropped something and the sudden clatter in the silent house made him almost lose his footing, made his heart race as he grabbed at the railing, and in his office he thought about pouring another small drink, but closed the drawer again. He had planned to spend the afternoon reading a few more chapters of Beard's book on neurasthenia, looking over the paper on galvanism in the new *Lancet*. May was usually the quietest month, the oldest and sickest of his patients already carried off by the long winter, children breathing easily, running out in the fresh air. But he knew there would still be people tapping at his door, maybe with some small complaint, maybe to settle a bill, but really to talk about the morning. When he opened the back door the air was soft on his face and the world was light and green. Not the muddy smell of the first of spring, but something gentler. He thought of putting the saddle on Prince, of galloping along any road that led out of town, but in the end he hitched up the buggy and they moved out more sedately. The door to Allen's store stood open but all the others along the north road were firmly closed and they flicked at the edge of his vision as he drove, some green, some fresh black, some weathered wood.

· · ·

Professor Harris had a daughter named Faith, who wore a shimmering, leaf-colored dress and sat with them at dinner, full of questions and opinions. And the Professor, the fierce Professor, smiled from the end of the table and told them about her Latin and Greek, about the work she did, collecting money and clothing, visiting the poor. *Very commendable,* Smith murmured, looking up quickly and then down at his plate again.

The dishes were gold rimmed and the wine glasses sparkled in the light of tall candles. Robinson, feeling that he could say anything at all, asked if she really believed that charity was the answer, if she didn't agree that however well intentioned, it merely allowed things to go on in their wretched state. *Please explain, Mr. Robinson,* Faith said, sounding suddenly like her father in the lecture room. So he asked if she really thought a man would work hard to better himself, his lot, if he knew he would be taken care of, regardless. It was true that there were deserving cases, they all knew that, but wouldn't she admit that they brought a great deal on themselves? So many children, for one thing, and money spent in the tavern instead of on food and clothing, on education. It was an opinion he'd heard Smith express many times, after a clinic at the hospital, but now Smith sat silent and with his own words lingering in the air Robinson suddenly wasn't sure if he believed them. They had come easily to his lips, an opinion he seemed to have acquired, although he couldn't remember ever thinking about it. He thought now of the ragged children pelting passersby with horse dung and running away, laughing. He thought of the taverns that lined the way he took from Marianne's house to his lodgings, the light and noise spilling into the street, the cursing bodies sometimes rolling out the door. The women who called out as he walked quickly home, inflamed by the kisses Marianne had allowed, and how once, cutting through an alleyway, he had heard an animal grunting, seen shapes moving against the sooty brick, hard to make out.

Mr. Robinson, Faith said, and he noticed a flush of red on her cheeks, noticed how much he minded the edge in her voice. The Professor raised a hand before she could continue, gave her a look that she obeyed. The serving girl carried in a platter of meat, refilled their glasses, and Smith commented on the wonderful meal. The Professor said that their cook was a treasure, and Faith picked up her silver fork, said, *Are you from the city, Mr. Robinson?* and he answered that he had lived there some years. *And what of your family?* she asked, and he said that he had none, and asked for the sauce to be passed.

.   .   .

There had been no rain for a week or more and the road was dry, but not yet swirling with dust. He turned down Blasted side road, with a vague idea of stopping at the McCains' to see how Simon's leg was healing. But Prince kept up a steady trot past the rutted lane and he settled himself as comfortably as he could on the seat, let the reins lie loose in his hands. Thinking, for some reason, of the doors along the north road flicking past. Thinking about doors, about opening a door, or sitting at a desk looking at one, how no one had ever said what that would be like. Not the Professor, not the others who came to the lecture rooms, who led them through the corridors of the hospital, dropping bloody dressings at the bedside. Some of the lecturers tried to prepare them, told stories from their own experience. Told them what it was like to do everything you could to save a man, a child, and to lose them anyway. And what it was like to see a boy who had been all but dead just hours before, out rolling a hoop with his friends. But no one mentioned waiting for a knock at the door, or the moment before it opened, no idea who or what would come through. The little thrum of anticipation, a challenge every time, a test of skill, of learning, a puzzle to be solved. He couldn't believe that he was the only one who saw it that way, still saw it that way, although as he grew older he sometimes felt apprehension, even dread, with his quickening pulse. When he first came to town, old Dr. Poole introduced him around, advised a notice in the newspaper, and Robinson wondered how much he'd been told. He shook men's hands, held Marianne's elbow going up the steps to church, sat in the freshly papered room in the new house and waited for the tap at the door, waited for the start of it all. Poor Miss Burns the first, he remembered, long dead now.

He slowed Prince to a walk, and could hear the buggy creaking. Some kind of bushes flowered wild by the side of the road, and a sweet rush of feeling filled him up. He wondered if anyone would watch over Heath, by the light of a tall candle, but knew it was unlikely. He was probably already closed in the box, the tap of the hammer, the nails biting cleanly, everything sealed up. Over. The lives he had taken avenged, as they had to be, and people ready to talk about other things. Heath had gone to wherever it was he was expected, although in fact he'd seemed to have left his life months before. When they took him in the woods there was one bullet left in the gun but he made no attempt to use it, on himself or on the men who knocked him down. Mostly he was silent, the sheriff said, sitting on his cot, staring at his feet on the floor. Heath answered Robinson's questions, during the monthly examinations, but only with a word or two, and never meeting his eyes. The same with the doctors his young lawyer brought from the city to determine his sanity. In the end Wellman could only argue that Heath must be insane, because only an insane man could do what he had done, but the jury was not convinced. That morning, just that morning, Robinson had thought that he might finally look up, might look him in the eye. He had realized that he was keeping his own eyes fixed on the white shirt beneath the dark gray coat, the loose threads dangling where two buttons were missing, maybe given as souvenirs to the jailers who stood by his side.

. . .

That day in September Robinson was tired, so tired, and thinking that it would have been wiser to take the bed that was offered at Radfords' farm. But once the crisis was past all he wanted was to be gone, to be out of the dark, creaking house, little more than a shack, where the children peeped over the edge of the loft, their eyes just dark smudges in pale faces. All he wanted was to lie down in his own soft bed.

The moon was still high but he was the only thing moving along the country road, the jingle of Prince's harness the only sound. The night wrapped around the leaves of the brooding trees and the way the moonlight brushed them only made them stranger; even Prince seemed to feel it, straining to go faster. But Robinson held him back, knowing what could happen. A bigger rut in the rutted road, the buggy overturned. Perhaps a broken leg, white bone showing, and lying on the hard-packed dirt for hours. Just before they reached the turn to the Emden road he sensed something to his left, saw dark shapes moving, close, but not close enough to hear. Horses, dark horses, maybe three, maybe four, moving past at a run, black tails streaming, picked out by the cold moon. Moving past them, and then gone. Silent, but a deeper silence after they'd passed, making him wonder if he *had* heard the sound of thundering hooves, or only expected to hear it. And he thought how odd it was, horses racing in the middle of the night, over unfenced land.

· · ·

The darkness was loosening as they finally came into town. He settled Prince and climbed the stairs, pulled back the covers, but each time he slid into sleep strange dreams arrived with a thump, and he had to get up again. The day, when it properly came, was blue and crisp and the morning passed, and in the dead part of the afternoon he was dozing in his chair when he heard pounding at the door, the front window rattling. Constable Street with a wild look in his eyes, hurrying him along the walk, up the two steps, through the gaping doorway. *The little girl,* he said. *She made a sound when I turned her over; she's still alive.* But she wasn't; later he explained the gasp, the gurgle, though Street didn't seem to take it in.

He'd never been in Heath's house, but it was laid out like many others, and even without Street's broad back in front of him he could have gone straight to Rachel's room. It was clear what had happened and he thought he could still smell a trace of gunpowder, but that may have been his fancy, looking at the wound. From the way she'd fallen it seemed she might have been kneeling at the side of the bed. He'd seen many things, but nothing as cold and hard as this, and he remembered that a day or two before he had seen her with Eaton, just outside the low gate, her hand stretched out to give

him something, and his stretched out to take it. He remembered
that innocent as that moment was it made him think, seeing his son
alone with a girl, of all that lay before him. He thought of his own
first fumblings, his ignorance and his terror, and thought that it
was almost time to explain things to Eaton, to give him facts to
ease his way. Maybe they would take fishing poles, just the two of
them, to a quiet spot on the river. In the spring, when it was warm
enough to roll their shirtsleeves up, and Lucy could pack them a
lunch and they would talk, man to man, father to son.

Street led him next to the back room, the one looking over
the yard, bare patches picked by the chickens, he supposed, although there were none to be seen. Along one side was a roughly
fenced section that looked like it might have been a garden, and
he knew there was something about that, something Lucy had
heard, but he couldn't remember what. It felt like he spent a long
time noticing these things, while his eyes moved to the shape lying wedged between the end of the bed and the plain wardrobe,
and though he knew it already, something lurched when he recognized the faded blue fabric of the dress Lilian usually wore.
He felt for her pulse, though it was clear there was no need,
thinking of all the times he'd done that. Thinking of the feeling
of her fragile life beneath his fingertips, gone now, as if it never
had been. *What in God's name happened?* he said, and Street said,
There's more, clearing his throat to get the words out.

Downstairs, Naomi lay by the pantry door, and she looked
so small. A bowl had smashed on the floor, maybe fallen, maybe
thrown, some kind of batter in hardened blobs and streaks on
the wall, on the table and the stove. *Heath?* he said, and Street
said, *Gone.*

· · ·

Later, much later, when Heath had been found and brought back to town, when Eaton had gone, white-faced, to bed, and Marianne's door had clicked shut, Robinson walked through the rooms of his house, turning down the lamps, and remembered the night horses. Marianne's mother had told him once, over the soup, of a night when she had woken with a start at the very moment that her own mother had died, something they learned only days later. He thought about his long drive back to town, the way Prince snorted and shook his head, the eerie way the moonlight stroked the trees and the silent horses thundering past. That was hours before the shots, but perhaps the very time Heath lay in the dark with open eyes, planning, deciding what he would do, and how he would do it. Though there was no reason he could think of that he would have slipped into Heath's world.

· · ·

Prince slowed as he lifted his tail, and Robinson thought how far he was from the life he'd assumed would be his. The life that would still have been his, at that moment when he lay on his bed with his hand held up before him, reciting the names of the bones. *Lunate, hamate, triquetrum.* That moment just before the tap at the door, when he couldn't have known how everything would change. He thought, in the days and weeks when he did nothing but think about it, that it had clearly been a test, and that he had failed. Not the test he thought it was, not a test of his compassion, but something else. There was a tap at the door, his landlady saying, *A young lady to see you,* and he picked up his jacket from the chair, smoothed his hair, looking in the crooked mirror. He assumed it would be Marianne, although she had never come to his rooms, but when he walked into the parlor Faith turned from the window and he was surprised at the sound of his voice, saying her name. *I need your help,* she said, looking past him to the half-open door.

Outside the air was dense with rain that had fallen, would fall again, and in the pearly light she stood out sharp beside him. But at the same time she was all softness, her pale brow, the pink of her cheek, and the beads of moisture that clouded her hair where it showed beneath her brown hat. As he walked beside her there seemed to be time to notice each small detail like that.

I need your help, Faith said again, and it was the usual story she told him. A young girl taken advantage of, a young girl in trouble. A good girl, a girl who worked hard, who would have a chance to find a good position, to have a decent life. *Can you say that it's right?* Faith said. *Can you honestly say that it's right?* This girl's life ruined, while the man carried on with his own, without even a pause.

He was persuaded, and he told himself it was by what she said, nothing to do with the misty look of her hair, with the fact that he was the one she had chosen to ask. The next day the note came with the address and he could have changed his mind, but he didn't. Remembering the way Faith had looked when he said yes, said he would help. The girl was thin and frightened, her small white teeth chattering. She held on to Faith's hand and there was blood, but not so much, not while he was still there. He never knew how the Professor learned of it, but that didn't really matter. Summoned to his office, Robinson felt like a schoolboy, braced for the whipping to come. The words fell hard, each one a dull thud landing, another piece of the golden path gone, a scatter of faint sparkles in the air, until they too disappeared. No question of the law, the Professor said, providing he left the city, set up somewhere far away and stayed there. A terrible mistake, the Professor said, with what he had been prepared to offer him. Robinson heard the trembling in his own voice as he made his brief responses, despised it but couldn't stop it. Even out in the street the blows continued, thudding with each beat of his heart, with the unbearable knowledge that he had only himself to blame.

He didn't tell Marianne any of it. An adventure, was what he said instead. An opportunity, a new start for their new life together. She thought he was teasing, at first. And when he made it clear that it was not a joke, that they would not be taking the house near the lake, that they would be living in a landlocked small town miles away, she wailed and stamped her pretty foot and told him he was hateful, told him that she never wanted to see him again. But the wedding was in two days' time, the house filled with flowers and the hem already finished on the dress. He sat on a chair on her front porch until it was nearly dark, and when she came out to him, he held both her hands and told her he would treasure her forever.

• • •

He woke to the sound of a shout, a cry, but the horse was standing peacefully, no sound but a distant bird. The reins were looped around the trunk of a sapling by the edge of the road; he must have done that, although he had no memory of it. Only the strange thought of his daughter's light skull cupped in his hand, nothing in him strong enough to bring her back. He pressed his fingers hard into his temples before he climbed down from the buggy, loosed the reins, stroked the horse's soft nose and looked into the dark pool of its eye. The sun was still high but its light had softened; he had misplaced his watch and had no idea how long he had slept. No idea if anyone had passed by and seen him there, what a man might be saying to his wife as he eased off his boots by the kitchen door.

· · ·

The Marianne he first knew had the bluest eyes and a way of holding her fingers over her mouth when she giggled. She asked his opinion on everything. Once, near the time they first met, she touched the sleeve of his jacket and said, *You must be very brave.* He had been speaking of the surgery he'd observed that morning, trying to describe it without offending, but at the same time enjoying her shivers, as she herself seemed to. There was no reason to think of that now, but he did, and knew that it had never been true. He thought of the wrinkled face of Miss Burns, the first to tap at his office door, and what it must have cost her to unlace, unbutton, to bare herself and show the shameful swelling under her arm. What she must have gone through before he'd even heard her name, alone in her little house, deciding.

And he thought of those times the diphtheria swept through, the parents whose children were carried off, sometimes every one. Watching at bedsides night after night, hardly able to stand, yet wiping at their reddened eyes and thanking him for his trouble, for all he'd tried to do. He remembered the man with the crushed leg, at the factory, conscious until he died and making jokes about the dance he was going to miss. Reverend Toller standing tall in his pulpit, but moving through the laneways at dusk, tapping at back doors to return some glittering object he'd found in one of his wife's hiding places. Even his own son screaming in his bed, his hair all spiked and the lamp throwing terrible shadows on the wall. Sometimes screaming louder when Robinson stood in the doorway, saying, *Hush, hush. It was only a dream*. Marianne lost in her powdered sleep, making him wonder how it was those nights he was away from home. Or how it was for Lilian, who could barely speak, barely meet his eye, yet came to him week after week, trusted him. Even Heath in his cell hearing the hammer blows ring out, knowing the exact hour of his death. Robinson knew that even the vows he had made as a ragged boy had nothing to do with bravery.

• • •

The music stopped for a moment when he opened the back door, then started again. A piece Marianne liked to play, although he couldn't just then put a name to it. The slow sad notes wrapped around him and he thought about stepping into the room, sitting down in the armchair, and listening to the end. He thought of touching her hair. Standing in the doorway he saw her rigid back and the way her skirts flowed over the piano stool. He carried on past, up the stairs, poured water into the bowl, dipped his hands and splashed. The slow sad notes still repeating and he dried his face more roughly than he needed to, had to smooth his mustache with the special comb Eaton had given him for Christmas. When he came noisily back down the stairs the music had stopped and the parlor was empty.

There was a folded paper on the polished hall table, a note from Lett, inviting him to supper at Blyth's Hotel. He went to the kitchen to tell Lucy and felt a little spurt of anger at the way she set her lips, dropping the potato she was peeling back into the mounded bowl. Another when she asked about Eaton, still quiet in his room. *Let him sleep,* Robinson said, his hand rough on his office door. He sat down at his desk and opened Beard's book but after a time realized that he hadn't really read anything. Stray sentences snagging his attention, dragging it down to a place far from the desk, the chair, the fingers turning pages. *Lightning never kills or even hurts unless it finds resistance in its path . . . They are without past or future, and only a dull present . . . What patients confidently expect to happen will be very likely to happen.*

He rubbed his face, gave his head a shake, and flipped forward to the chapter of illustrative cases, hoping to find something of interest. Beard's Illustrative Case XI was a man of thirty, troubled by weekly emissions, by sweating hands, red spots on the forehead, by catarrh of the stomach. He reported that as a boy of seven he used to climb trees, and on so doing experienced sexual sensations, mingled pleasure and pain. He told Beard that he was so much annoyed by this that he gave up the habit of climbing entirely, although it had been what he had most loved to do. Case XIV was a gentleman who suffered from attacks of intense pain and heat behind the ears, and who also experienced palpitations of the heart when playing a game of cards or billiards. He could not bear the touch, even the thought, of flannel to the skin, and was afraid to use a public or a private privy or water closet. This gentleman was successfully treated with a course of bromide of potassa and tonics of quinia, strychnia and iron.

Robinson turned the page, but the ticking of the clock began to interfere. It sat on the corner of his desk, black and heavy with a porcelain face, a bronze figure on top. A man with an old-fashioned frock coat, knee breeches, one hand on his hip and the other held straight at his side. The clock was Marianne's gift on their wedding day; she'd had a brass plate fixed to the base, engraved with the date, and *Always*. He had given her a necklace on a delicate gold chain. Stood behind her doing up the clasp, dipped his face to her scented neck. That was in the high room in the grand hotel near the station, Marianne astonishing him with her delight, now that it was permitted. Making him laugh, her tangled hair tumbling down her back.

• • •

He closed the book and placed it on the little pile of journals not yet read. Wiped a few smudges from his desk, polished the face of the clock with the soft cloth he kept in the bottom drawer, with the bottle and glass. It was time he left, but he was thinking about other cases Beard's methods had cured, women living in misery until they walked through his door. Thinking of women in beds and on couches, women sitting on the hard chair in his own office. So many women, their eyes rimmed red from crying; there was a time when it seemed that Marianne's tears alone would be enough to sweep him away. At first it was some slight in a shop or an invitation not given; Robinson was all sympathy for as long as his patience lasted, trying to understand how a cold look from a woman she hadn't yet met could be a tragedy in her world. From her sobbing sentences he came to see that she had pictured herself arriving in Emden like royalty, stepping down from the carriage in her dress of the latest fashion, bringing her knowledge of concerts, of entertainments, of how to live a civilized life. Certain that she was just the person the town had been sleepily waiting for, that her opinion would be eagerly sought, that cards would pile up on the new silver tray. But the town was neither as backward nor as biddable as she had assumed, the order already firmly established, and all he could think of was to give her money for new dresses, for a dining table shipped from England, a new set of dishes painted with tiny pink flowers.

More tears with the gouts of blood that were their children, refusing to stay, and each time more days, more weeks in the darkened room. He worried about her not eating, told the girl who worked for them then to make up sweet, rich things, cakes and pastries, airy loaves of bread that could be thickly spread with butter. He carried up the silver tray with its scatter of visiting cards and she stirred them with her pale fingers, closed her eyes again. At some point he had moved to the room across the hall, so as not to disturb her when he was called out at night, and somehow he never moved back to their high, carved bed.

· · ·

He felt a gritty tiredness in his eyes as he moved down the street, thought briefly of sending an excuse to the hotel, of lying down on cool sheets and sinking into a deep, dreamless sleep. He thought of Eaton, who would still be in his bed when the sun was high if Lucy didn't climb the stairs to waken him, and with that thought remembered that he had meant to look in again before he left the house. There was a baseball game sometime soon, he would take him to that; they would sit side by side and cheer for the Maple Leafs. It would be good for Eaton, a noisy crowd, fresh air. It would be good for both of them.

As he passed the corner of Powell Street he met a group of men coming up the hill from the factory, nodded to their greetings, and thought about the fact that he knew almost every face in Emden, that he was part of the town in a way he never would have imagined when he first shook Dr. Poole's hand. He had hoped at that time that it might still be a temporary banishment. Some years, maybe five years, and then surely all would be forgotten, forgiven. Not the end of his golden road after all, but a side track that would join up again. It wasn't a hope that he remembered setting aside, but he was quickly busy, long days and nights and drives through the countryside, until he was enmeshed in the town, tangled in other lives. Some years ago he had read the Professor's obituary in the city paper, read that he was survived by his daughter, Faith, and for days he had thoughts that he had to tamp down.

Behind him he could hear the men needling someone who was going directly home, most of them veering off to Pond's tavern, or Malley's. No doubt giving a saucy greeting to Sarah Barnes, who would be stationed outside the door, her eyes fierce behind her spectacles, leaflets in her clenched hands. He had been called often enough to the factory to know what kind of day those men had spent, but they walked with easy steps, some with arms about each other's shoulders. Robinson knew almost every face in the town; there were men he talked with, shared a cigar with, men he was glad to run into on the street or at a meeting table. But he realized there was no one he would ever walk with in that easy, unthinking way, maybe never had been. He and Smith had been close for a time, with their shared trials and aspirations, but only for a little while. Smith was in Montreal, maybe had been for years, something Robinson only knew from reading the articles on contagion he occasionally contributed to the *Medical Record*.

He thought of Eaton and the O'Neill boy, sticks clattering in their rolling hoops, and the way he sometimes saw them running and whooping through the long waving grass in Badgers' Field. He must have had friends like that, when he was a boy in that other place, but he couldn't summon a memory of any. All that came was a picture, the rough bark of a tree, up close, lit by blazing sun. A slender caterpillar, an inchworm, bright green like the color of new leaves, making its slow, deliberate way upward. Pausing at each gnarled spot, the front part of its body flailing free in the air until it adjusted to the different surface, came down flat and continued on its way. A boy's hand reaching, grubby, broken fingernails, flicking it away, and he didn't think it was his own hand, but he didn't really know.

．　．　．

How could he not know if it was his own stained finger or someone else's, flicking the caterpillar away to be crushed beneath a cracked boot sole, or maybe for the pleasure of watching it start again, watching it struggle again and again. The kind of casual cruelty that Robinson saw everywhere, some days of his life, along with the more calculated kind. The way of a man like Lett, with his ruddy cheeks, his booming laugh. The very picture of jovial good nature, but ruthless in ways that Robinson knew, and ways he'd heard about. Married to Marl's plain-faced daughter, Lett ran the factory, owned property in all four corners of the town and half the center block, sat on every committee there was. A finger in every pie, he liked to say, bullying and pushing through his scheme for a competing railway line, which was good for the town, in the end, but better for Lett, better for Marl, who stayed in the shadows in his big house on the hill.

Lett was a great talker at his dinner table, in meeting rooms, but he had nothing to say about the men who couldn't hold out until the railway profits came through. Nothing to say about the new dry goods merchant who came to town with his wife and young family, who left a year later, a broken man. The fire that took most of his stock finished him off, and Lett was right there to buy the building lot with its mounds of blackened timbers, broken glass. Paying a fair price, perhaps, considering the condition, but far from a good price. Right there again to bail out Heath the night he was arrested, although that was an odd thing. Heath was Marl's bookkeeper, after all, for the factory and his other interests, and it was Marl who had brought the embezzlement charge, sent the constables immediately to his door. There'd be a reason for it, maybe some kind of lesson being taught, but Robinson didn't care to puzzle it out. The business of living complicated enough, he thought, and harm done for enough plain reasons without having to dream up new, twisted ones.

There were other things Robinson knew about Lett, among them a condition treated more than once, like one or two others who sang the Sunday hymns with great feeling and supported the movement to ban communion wine. In some ways, he thought, it was easier to deal with a man like Brendan O'Neill, everything plain to see. Hot tempered when he had been drinking, and he had usually been drinking. Lashing out at anyone who was near. His wife, before she took sick, was almost as hard. Had once swung an iron skillet and laid Brendan out flat on the floor, sent for Robinson because she thought maybe she'd killed him, although she was still too angry to be much bothered about it. She was half her own size now, paring away to nothing. Those wild, hulking sons talking softly in the tiny rooms of their house. The one that was Eaton's friend kept the hard-packed floor swept, washed plates in a tin tub by the crooked front door. Stuffed a clutch of purple flowering weeds into a jar on the sill beside her bed. *He's a good boy,* she said, and Robinson thought she was probably right. Wondered if the two of them knowing it would be enough.

There were many who wouldn't agree, but Robinson didn't mind that Eaton ran off with the O'Neill boy to the woods, to the river, whenever he could. Even after the thrown stone, Meyer losing his eye to a jagged piece of the overturned wagon. He still thought that it would be good for his son to learn a little toughness, to have more of the rough and tumble of a boy's life along with his other lessons. Marianne insisted on tidiness and good manners, the weekly Band of Hope meetings, and there was nothing wrong with that. But there was more involved in becoming the right kind of man, something to do with scraped knuckles and bloodied noses, with taking chances. The thought of his son swinging out on a rope over the deep green river or playing dare on the railroad tracks still clenched his heart, brought pictures of bodies crushed and slashed, a shock of hair stiffened into icy spikes above a small drowned face. He could only trust that it was something like the story of Abraham, that he had to be prepared for a sacrifice that would not, in the end, be required.

Robinson knew many fathers of sons, and most of them had an idea of the future. A path long mapped out, someone to follow in their footsteps, to take their place in a business and eventually step aside for their own sons. He had maybe thought that too at one time, taking Eaton along on long country rounds, teaching him the position of the organs in the body, the names of the instruments in his bag. But more and more as he sank, bone weary, into his chair, his bed, he wondered why he would wish this life on anyone, let alone his clear-eyed son. Alice Barnes said that Eaton had a fine, inquiring mind, told Robinson that much as she would hate to lose him, she thought it was time to send him on to the Grammar School, to others who could teach him more. She said he had a keen sense of justice, of fairness, that perhaps he was destined for the law. *I can see him in the courtroom,* she said, and for a moment Robinson could too. As Eaton grew older, grew into himself, it happened sometimes that Robinson caught a glimpse of his adult face. A face something like his own, in the shape of the chin, the way the brown hair lay, though the blue eyes were his mother's. A glimpse of Eaton grown, maybe with a pen in his hand, or swinging a child up onto his broad shoulders, a glimpse of him even older; at times when Eaton sat reading his schoolbooks Robinson saw a shadow of a face so old that he knew that he himself was long gone, and he was swept with an almost unbearable sadness.

It happened the other way too, some movement bringing such a clear picture of Eaton stumbling on learning legs, holding tight to his hand. He had the fanciful thought that each person moved around with the shades of themselves in the past and the future, the seed both foretelling the tall standing flower and contained within it. Talking to Alice Barnes, in front of Allen's store on a drowsy afternoon, he remembered the girl with flying skirts, the way she and her sister Sarah, looking so alike, would pinch and kick at each other all through church, pull each other's hair in rages on their front walk. He remembered their father saying that he'd have to get them married off early, more trouble than a whole herd of boys.

Andrew Barnes was a man he had liked, a man who might have become the kind of friend he was thinking about, if he had lived a little longer. Mrs. Lewis sent a cab to bring Robinson to Neeve Street one still Christmas night, when the snow fell in fast, soft flakes. Upstairs in her tall, narrow house, Barnes lay dead on an iron bed. *His heart, was it?* Mrs. Lewis said from the doorway, while Robinson lifted back the thin sheet, checked the cooling body, and he told her that it seemed so. *How long ago?* he asked, and she said that it had been a little while, that she'd had to clear the house, find a boy to go for the cab. But he'd been dead as a doornail, beyond saving, she was quite sure of that.

There were those, Robinson knew, who would have crammed Barnes back into his clothes, dumped him somewhere in the snow, maybe even in front of another establishment. But Mrs. Lewis knew the law, knew that nothing could be proved against her. The doctor called, her three nieces fast asleep in their beds, and no business of hers to ask why a man would want a room in her lodging house with his own fine place just blocks away.

Robinson had been there before, the first time to see a girl raving on a couch, her cheeks flaming with fever. That was when he was newly arrived in the town and didn't know, didn't think anything of walking up to the front door in the broad light of day. Mrs. Lewis was a stout woman, white-haired now and plainly dressed, looking like anyone's mother. A kindly seeming woman, but with iron at the core. The kindness was real, Robinson knew that, but knew too that she never let it get in the way of things. Not so different, in that way, from many he could name.

The fevered girl had recovered but her wits were affected and Mrs. Lewis sent her back to her people. Sent her somewhere, at any rate. She didn't like her girls to go about much in town and so Robinson came to the house from time to time, when one of them needed attention. She always offered him a glass, a cup of tea, and he occasionally accepted, sinking into a plush chair in a parlor that looked almost like any other. Mrs. Lewis knew what she could and could not ask of him and made other arrangements if she needed to, although there was rarely a problem like that in her house. Almost as if a child could not be conceived without love, although he knew that was far from true. More to do with the douches and infusions, the sponges and tents and mixtures of ergot, tansy, knowledge that Mrs. Lewis shared in the dim parlor, speaking in a voice that could have been telling him the price of a bolt of cloth. It was information Robinson himself sometimes passed on, presenting it as something he'd come across in his latest medical journal. For so many pale women, there was little else he could do.

Once, when it was gin they were sipping in the comfortable chairs, she told Robinson that she thought they were rather similar, and not just in their helping professions. She said she was thinking more of the way they both knew too many secrets to ever be completely welcome, outside their own doors. Another time she sent a note to Robinson's house, the name and direction of a farmer one of her girls had clawed in the face. It was a face the girl knew from years before, when she was a slip of a thing in a faded dress, stepping off a boat and being lifted up into his wagon. He'd had a wife then, who was waiting at the farmhouse door. Maybe still did, not that that made any difference.

Attacking a customer was not something Mrs. Lewis would ever have tolerated, except that Junie was one of her best girls ever, and she knew there must have been powerful reasons. To calm her down, Mrs. Lewis promised to find out if he still lived in the badly chinked house at the edge of the swamp, find out if he'd changed his ways. The next day, Robinson bumped up the rutted track, knocked at the blistered front door that faced nothing but stony fields. Found Abby in a mucky, dark room, and took her home with him.

·   ·   ·

The main dining room at Blyth's was half full when Robinson arrived and he nodded to more familiar faces but kept walking through. When he opened the door to the private room a falsetto voice was saying, *But sir, me mother told me*— and he was slapped by a wave of laughter, pulled with it as it rolled back, and released at the last empty chair. It was a round table, but somehow Lett was at the head, Jervis at his right hand, still laughing although it had been his put-on voice telling the joke. Jervis had made a fool of the defense lawyer at the trial, turning his words, shifting the tone and firing them back at him. Wellman was an earnest young man from the city, with spectacles and an untamed cowlick. Hired by someone, maybe even Lett or Marl, to do the impossible. He had scuttled away as soon as the verdict was read, still cramming papers into his bag as he walked toward the station.

The walls of the small room were newly papered, the gas fixtures elaborately scrolled. No sign of the sweeping arm of temperance here; someone filled his glass to the brim and told him he'd have to down it quickly to catch up. Looking around the table, he saw how true that was. Spence, the banker, with his jacket off, McAdam's collar undone. It was McAdam's young clerk who had sold Heath the gun, wrapped it in brown paper as requested. He couldn't have known, even McAdam himself couldn't have known, but he let the boy go anyway, sent him off with a good recommendation and a week's wages in his pocket.

Luft was saying that he'd already written his front page, lacked only a statement from the hangman, last seen running toward the stables. *A bad business,* Robinson said, and everyone nodded. They had all been there, had all seen it, heard the awful noises that came from beneath the dark hood, but at the same time were everywhere around them. *Bad enough to execute the poor mad bastard,* Luft said, and from across the table Jervis said, *Ah, will you leave it.*

But Luft wouldn't leave it, the two of them getting louder and louder until Jervis banged his glass, amber sloshing over the rim, and counted off the points on his fingers, much as he had done in the courtroom. One: Heath was sane enough to make a devious plan. Two: the plan was clearly made ahead, coldly followed through. Buying the gun on credit before news of the charge had time to spread, sending the older girl for the music, taking the little one out of school. Three: he fled; he was sane enough for that. He tried to escape, not like that madwoman from up near Blasted, the one who took an ax to her man and then just sat down at the edge of the stony field, smeared with his blood, until some poor soul happened by. *You remember that, Robinson?* he said, and Robinson did. *And finally,* Jervis said, *if you think about it, it was in fact a very sane act. He'd have gone to prison, wouldn't he, for the embezzlement. Wouldn't he,* Jervis repeated, looking at Lett, who nodded. *And what would have become of his womenfolk?* Jervis said. *No money, no family to help them. It would have been the Poor-house, wouldn't it? That's what I mean by sane. Sane enough to make a choice, to know what their fate would be without him.*

There are worse things than the Poor-house, Luft said, and Jervis shook his head, said, *Not many.*

They wouldn't have survived it, Spence said. *My wife said the older girl was so simple she could barely speak, the mother a meek little thing. When she saw them about in the town, you know.*

And if he was mad, McAdam said, *there would have been some sign. My clerk said he was cool as could be, quite as usual. Aren't I right, Robinson?* he said. *Let's have your opinion, wouldn't someone have noticed if he was mad?*

Most likely, Robinson said, but he was thinking of something he'd read in Beard's book that very afternoon, started to tell them about it. A class of patients Beard called *Border-liners,* who were almost insane at times, or even all of the time, but never quite enough to justify a diagnosis. A happily married woman, perfectly normal except for her calmly stated belief that some gnawing creature lived inside her right leg. A man who slapped his own face, hard enough to mark, whenever he heard church bells. *As for the girl,* Robinson said, *she was suffering from a disease, poor thing.* He told them that the course of therapy he had devised was beginning to prove successful, that given a little more time he firmly believed that she could have lived a normal life. Normal enough.

There you have it, McAdam said. *The voice of modern medicine.* He seemed content, although Robinson wasn't sure what point he thought had been proved.

A long way from old Dr. Poole's day, Lett said, and everyone laughed. Spence put on a raspy, quavering voice, said, *The problem clearly stems from a disturbance in the bowels. Purgatives for one and all,* Luft said, raising his glass, and Jervis told a story about consulting Dr. Poole about pain in his stomach, the day before his first big trial. The Epsom salts he was given seemed to help and before leaving for the courthouse he took a triple dose, with predictable results.

·   ·   ·

Robinson's glass was full again and he noticed that his fog of fatigue had blown away. He was suddenly very hungry and just as he realized that, the door opened and Blyth himself appeared, carrying a tray of steaming plates, a boy behind him with several bottles. It seemed important to mention the coincidence, but Spence had begun a complicated joke or story about a farmer and a spotted cow and Robinson found himself laughing with the others, mostly at the way Spence mangled the telling. McAdam laughed loudest and longest and Robinson remembered something he'd heard, an argument over a loan the banker had not given, or called in early. He wondered if it was really possible to leave business at the door, couldn't imagine his own life, if his work was the same. He'd known them all for years, Lett and

Spence and McAdam, Jervis and Luft. He'd sat with them on rickety stages, at ceremonies and prize-givings. Spoken with them on the street, examined some behind the closed door of his office. But he'd never been with them all in a room like this, leaning back in their chairs, easy together. He thought of his tipsy conversation in Mrs. Lewis' parlor, thought that she had been wrong, for here he was at this round table, the things he knew not any kind of barrier. Across from him Lett raised his glass, and Robinson lifted his own, and drank.

· · ·

There was not much talk while they ate and he found he was thinking of the farmer, the woman he hadn't seen but had been told about, blood on her hands and face, spattered all over her dress. He knew the place, might even have seen the ax, leaning by the door, although it was years before, possibly not the same ax. The words *New Home* were written on the ragged hem of the shift Abby had been wearing and he had sent an angry letter, received by return post a reply from Miss Augusta Weir who was distressed, appalled, who assured him that no more girls would be sent to Ashfield's farm. She enclosed the fare to send the girl back but it didn't seem right to ship her off like a parcel, and at the time he was far too busy to take her himself. From the first she was very good with Eaton and quick to learn the household details Marianne showed her, and she was cheerful enough after the first few days. Robinson wrote again to Miss Weir saying they would keep her, asked about her history, if she had any family living. There was a brother, apparently, who had been sent to the West, and a sister who had also been placed, after a great deal of difficulty. Miss Weir suggested that the information not be passed on until Abby was older and he thought about that, decided that if she asked, he would tell her what he knew, help her to find out more. But she didn't ask, and he thought that was to her credit. The way she fit herself into a new life, the way she was able to leave the past completely behind.

Abby had been with them for years before she began to disturb his sleep, before he woke from a dream of his hand cupped over her bare breast, his fingers trickling down her thigh. He despised himself, the things he couldn't stop noticing. The movement of her skirts when she bent to the oven door, the flush in her cheeks when she stood up again. He despised his thoughts, the excuses he found to seek her out in the quiet kitchen, once Marianne had climbed the stairs. The way he was driven half mad imagining rumpled sheets on her narrow, sweet-smelling bed. It was wearing him out, this control, and he was sorry, knew that she was hurt when he arranged a new place. Knew that his voice was too hard, explaining that Eaton was old enough now, that Mr. Cowan, old and frail, needed her more, that it would better suit her.

After Cowan died, she found employment in young Ryan's studio and Marianne tutted, but Robinson saw it a different way. Proof that Abby would be all right, that she would always pick herself up and start again, go on with the life he could so easily have interfered with. He was glad of that, happy to see her occasionally when she came to visit Lucy, but in a proper way. In the way he had felt when she was a bony, trembling child, carried safe in his arms.

· · ·

The boy cleared away the smeared plates and brought another decanter, a box of cigars Lett must have requested. Rolling one between his thin fingers, Jervis told a story of being in Daly's once, waiting behind Heath who was inspecting each type of cigar. *I didn't know who he was,* Jervis said, *not then. But I couldn't help noticing him, the cut of his coat, the boots that had seen better days. But carrying on like a lord, asking the price of a box of this one and that. Well, he left with a single, of course, and even then he had to count out coppers. Daly and I had quite a laugh about it, after he'd gone.*

McAdam said that there had been a story going around that Heath was, in fact, a lord or an earl or some such thing, sent away from his estate in disgrace, and Robinson said he remembered his wife saying something like that. *That's all it was,* Spence said. *A story the women passed around, like something out of one of their novels. Not a jot of truth in it—ask Lett.*

Lett spoke through a haze of bluish smoke, said, *No rich blood there, that's certain. He came from Liverpool latterly, as far as we know. Our man talked to his old employer—no, the son of his old employer. A brickyard, it was.* Lett said that the son didn't know the details, only that there had been some dishonesty. Also some kind of family tragedy, a child dying, maybe even two children, and the old man took pity; otherwise Heath would surely have been jailed. It was before his time there, but the son thought his father had paid passage to Canada instead, said he was soft like that. *There were one or two still at the yard who remembered him,* Lett said, *but only vaguely. No idea of his background, where he had been before. Maybe we could have found out more, made further inquiries, but we decided there was no point in it.* He waved his hand to indicate and knocked the platter the serving boy was lifting away. A long, ugly piece of gristle landed on Lett's shoulder, slithered down his sleeve, and something chased over his face before Spence began to laugh, before he joined in. The boy left quickly, things rattling in his hands, and

Jervis began another joke, one that Robinson had heard him tell before. Beside him, Luft was saying something, and Robinson noticed that he had to blink to bring the face into focus, had to strain to hear the words that slipped under the loud laughter from the other side of the table. Something about bootstraps, he thought, and Lett. Something about Luft telling his own son that he could do anything, be anything he wanted. *Interesting, isn't it?* Luft said, and Robinson nodded, watching the fingers, permanently ink-stained, as they straightened a fork on the wine-stained cloth. *Interesting that we seem to have nothing but scorn for the wretch we hanged today, mock him for ideas above his station, all of that.*

What are you saying? Robinson asked, blinking again. But Luft just shook his head, called over to McAdam and drew attention to his empty glass.

· · ·

The room was becoming very warm, faces shiny and all jackets now off, collars undone. McAdam had just finished a song about a bonny lass, banging time on the edge of the table, and Spence was trying to sing a song of his own, his body convulsing with violent hiccups, the rest of them laughing until their sides ached. Everything was wonderful and Robinson thought, *Like this, let me stay like this.*

For some reason he thought of something he'd read out to Eaton, a foreign item in the newspaper. They were building a tower in Paris, and it was already so high that the men working on top enjoyed sunshine, while fog and mist prevailed below. That's what it felt like, something like that, basking in warmth and everything so clear. Everything he saw, even the edges of the door, the way it opened slowly, the wary look on the boy's spotty face as he came in with two more bottles. There was something about doors, he knew there was something about doors that had been nagging at him, and watching the boy's cautious entrance he knew what it was, so clear, so simple. There were two sides to every door, that was it, that was important, and someone stood outside, someone in, and it was something to do with that. This thing about doors that was nagging.

He remembered remembering his first days in Emden, sitting at his desk, the new clock ticking, looking at the door and wondering who would first come through. His landlady's tapping before that, and himself inside, *lunate, hamate, triquetrum,* on the verge of a different life. He remembered learning the sound of Lilian's knocking, the first time thinking it the scratching of some small animal, and he remembered that while he was certain of his diagnosis, it sometimes seemed that all that was really wrong with her was a profound, unbearable sadness. He suddenly saw how easy it had been for him, asking his questions, making his notes, sending her on her way with encouraging words. How easy the compassion, the involvement, all of it easy, even the sleepless nights, the bedside vigils. He thought of old Miss Burns again, of the praying calluses on Mrs. Toller's knees.

It had something to do with doors and he remembered a splintered, foul-smelling staircase, the terrible fear on a young girl's face as he stepped into the tiny room, Faith rising from the one chair to thank him. He thought of Marianne behind her closed door, instead of himself outside it. Thought of what Eaton saw, rousing from a nightmare, seeing his door slowly open, black leaping shadows in the lamp glow. His child, his only child, and he thought of all the others, conceived out of love and youth and hope, the ones who refused to stay. Thought of Eleanor, who so nearly did. What did it mean that the only survivor was his beautiful son, made from drunkenness and rage and despair.

That's what it had been, it was clear to him now, in his quiet space inside the swirl of noise and heat and hard laughter. It hadn't seemed so at the time, that memory still with him, although he had done his best to put it aside. Late at night and restless, the bottle and the glass, trying to read in his chair, pacing the room, sitting down, then pacing again. Thoughts racing in his head and then out of the spin of them a memory, a picture of Marianne's smile, of her hand on his sleeve, and a sudden understanding that he was wrong, that it had all been wrong, his solicitude, his restraint, and he knew, he suddenly knew how to get it all back. And then his hand was on the door, the flowery scent of Marianne's room, her hair spread out around her lovely face, against the white of the pillow. So long since he had seen her like that, so long since they had laughed through the curtains of her hair and he was overwhelmed by love, he was overwhelmed and he had to tell her, had to show her, her pushing hands meant nothing because he knew how to make it right, he knew how to bring it all back, he did. But later, when he touched her face, his hand slipped through her tears.

· · ·

He found himself in the street and his thoughts were moving faster than his feet, or maybe it was his feet stepping ahead of his thoughts. Something, at any rate, was not working properly with something else, so he stood completely still, and waited. The street was dark and quiet and he fumbled at his pocket, his fingers moving slowly enough for his mind to recall that his watch was still missing. For a moment it seemed very important to know what the time was and he turned to see if the lights from Blyth's were still up full, but that was a mistake. The spinning made him remember that there had suddenly been no air in the private room, made him remember Spence's gray head resting on the table, a lock of his hair, just the tip of it, lying in a puddle of something that had spilled. A rush of sound and then only his own blood pumping, filling up his ears. Reddened faces, mouths opening and closing, but only the sound of his own heart's work. And now he was in the empty street and he roped in his scattering thoughts, tried to make them address the problem of his feet, making one move, then the other, trying to get them into a rhythm they could continue on their own. His shoulder bumped against a hard surface and he leaned into it for a moment, knowing that there was something he was forgetting, something that he had suddenly known in the heaving room he had left behind. His fingertips knew that they touched rough stone as he pushed himself straight, pushed a little too hard but caught himself, righted himself. He would have to think about the important thing later, he would, but first he had to get to the end of this empty street, round the corner, face another long, dark road.

· · ·

There was something important and he had the feeling that it was something familiar, that he'd been here before, more than once, been in the moment just after he'd understood the important thing. It seemed that time was also in disarray, the end of the block was no closer but when he looked down at his feet they appeared to be stepping along quite smartly, propelling him straight ahead, still straight ahead while the rest of his body leaned into the corner he had arrived at unexpectedly. He wasn't aware of falling, but down on the ground he thought it would be nice to close his eyes and rest a little, and he might have done that. Singing voices spilled out of Malley's, somewhere nearby, and he knew that for some reason it was not a good thing to be lying facedown in the dirt so he pushed himself up, his hand slipping wetly the first time he tried. It wasn't good to lie flat in the dirt and that had something to do with the hoarse, singing voices, with the top curve of Eaton's ear, his soft brown hair above the pulled-up blanket. He remembered riding out with his boy on a round of visits, telling him about sickness, about accidents, and Eaton saying, *But who takes care of you?*

Robinson's feet were moving faster but he didn't know if they would keep on. He knew that at that moment he would have given all the tea in China to have Marianne cradle his head in her hands, to have her stroke his brow and say, *Hush now. There there.* Then he thought about China for a little while, trying to remember if it was a real place. He tried to keep thinking about China instead of thinking about the steaming plates on the tray Blyth carried, the boy behind him with angry pustules on his face, the taste of roasted meat in his mouth, Lett's glistening chin. It was no use and the picket fence wobbled beneath his wet hand as he leaned over and retched, everything that he held splatting onto the colorless bush on the other side.

·   ·   ·

Better, much better, although he was still thick-fingered, fumbling for his handkerchief, wiping at his mouth, his mustache. Thinking about how the dark took the color from everything, how the best that the cold moon could show was shades of gray. He remembered the galloping horses and thought that they might not have been black at all, and for some reason that made him feel easier, although he'd had no idea they were still moving somewhere in his mind. But then he thought that it made no difference what color the horses really were, even *if* they were; he had seen them, seen them black. That thought went away when he brought the handkerchief down from his mouth and saw it was blotched dark, his hand too. A wound somewhere, a cut, and he wrapped the cloth tight around his hand, one more thing he would have to tend to before he could finally sleep.

Looking around, he realized that he had stumbled right past his own house, not even recognized it in the bleaching moonlight. He had left his bloody palm print on the Barnes' whitewashed fence but there was nothing he could do about that, although he had a brief idea that he should knock on the door, should say he was sorry, just sorry. He would have done it, but the house was dark; they were asleep, all of them, Alice and Sarah, their lonely mother whose name he couldn't remember. Turning his head, he saw that all the houses were dark, saw all the dark houses in lines everywhere, everyone silently sleeping, even the spirits behind the Heaths' boarded windows, and he understood that he was the only one awake, the only guardian. Too tired to let the thought do more than flicker, to wonder what would happen when he was gone. For he would be gone, soon enough. He would begin to move soon enough, his feet would obey, and his hand would open his own front door. He would climb the stairs as quietly as he could, find his bed and close his eyes, slip into his place in the dreams they all were dreaming. Leaving only the dark houses lining all the empty streets, only the cold, constant light of the indifferent moon.

BUTTON

THERE'S NOTHING REMARKABLE about it. Color of old bone, size of a small coin, holes for thread to pass through. It's only where it comes from that gives it meaning, and how long will that last? It may be kept in a small tin box for a generation or two, and then someone will want or need the box for something else. Hold the small button in the palm of a hand, half remembering a passed-down story, and put it into another container, a jar, maybe, for safekeeping. Doing that, but at the same time wondering if there really was a story, thinking that even if there was, it might not have been true. It may have come from one of those posed in the battered album that has also been passed down, faces faded or darkened with age, people with names no one alive still knows. And why assume that they always told the truth? Still, the button goes into a glass jar and someone thinks, late at night, of the way that stories lose their meaning, just like objects do, as the years wheel on, as new ones take their place. Someone understands that this thought too will be gone and no one will know, no one will ever know.

And perhaps sometime later, someone else will find a glass jar with one bone-colored button, add a few more. Maybe with a pinprick of a thought, or maybe the story is completely gone, although there are others. Over time the jar will fill up because that's the thing about buttons, they are always falling off, they are always turning up in a house, in a life, and you don't throw them away; there will surely come a day when you need just that color, just that size. The first small button is probably still rattling around in a jar with many others, old ones, newer, all shades and sizes, bits of trailing thread. Nothing at all to set it apart; it could have belonged to anyone.

LONG EXPOSURE

BEFORE I OPEN my eyes I hear the river, and I know that I'm waking up in his bed. Not yet dawn, but I can tell that it's near by the way I can just make out the shape of the chair where our clothes are piled, the long, inky band that must be one of my stockings. Before I knew Sam I would have thought, *It's dark*, but now I see the shades of it. Know that if I keep my eyes on it that chair will begin to emerge, slowly but ever steadily, until it is finally just there, the thing that it always was. I should get up; I should be gone before there's anyone about to see me carefully closing the back door. But it's warm in his bed, there's the sound of the river and the sound of his breath, and I turn and curl myself around him, my cheek on the smooth skin of his back, I breathe in the smell of him and all that is more important than what anyone might say.

· · ·

In Liverpool, before everything happened, we all slept together and if one of us complained that someone was kicking, that someone was pulling at the blanket, our mother would say we were lucky to have a bed at all. The little ones didn't know, some of them not yet born, but my brother Frank and I remembered the cellar room before. Only our blanket between us and the hard earth, and the water that slid down the walls. It was true what our mother said, that things could always be worse.

Sometimes I still catch myself thinking she will find us. Sail across the ocean and gather us up, tap at my door with the baby in her arms. It's a silly thought; for one thing, the baby would not be a baby anymore, would be older than I was when Miss Weir came. It used to be that I could hear my mother's voice when I thought of her. Just like I could see her face, and never gave a thought that it was something that could fade away, like the photographs Sam showed me, that hadn't been properly fixed. Only an outline left, sometimes just the trace of an eyebrow. At the very first, I saw her everywhere. Walking down the street ahead of us when we left Miss Weir's in our straggling line, or standing outside if I looked down from a high window. In the rumbling crowd waiting for the big ship, and even at New Home. Maybe that's what happened, maybe it's because of all those false mothers, the mistakes I made. Some just the shape of her, or wearing a shawl like her faded one, a way of turning their heads. Maybe they all jumbled up in my mind and erased my own real mother. Maybe it was my fault, maybe I should have known.

. . .

Yesterday morning they hanged the murderer Heath, and one of the jailers told Sam that for a consideration he would let him in to photograph the body, before they nailed down the box. Sam said that would make him no better than Taylor, who tried to get into the house while the bodies were still on the floor. Instead, the plates I developed show the crowd outside the jail, all gazing in the same direction. A few closer views of women with baskets, a stooped old man who looks to be shaking a stick at a tree. They could be gathered for any reason at all, maybe a parade or a revival meeting, and if someone saw them, years from now, they would have no idea.

Sometimes Sam is asked to take photographs of dead children, and though he has never said, I think that is why he taught me to use the dark-room so soon. He does it well; they look like they are sleeping, those children who shimmer in the fixing bath. They look like they have said their prayers and closed their eyes, never dreaming that they really would die before they woke. There are one or two in town who just appear when they hear that a child has gone, but Sam waits to be sent for. He can't afford to turn down any work, but he always hopes that word won't come. It feels so wrong, Sam says, setting up his camera in the hush of a grieving house, asking for the drapes to be opened wide. He says he doesn't understand why anyone would want to remember their child that way, but I think I do.

Most of our sitters are alive though, and most of them come to the house, and take their places on the red plush settee or on one of the rickety chairs. Sam is still a little cheaper than the other photographers in town and mostly it's families that come, stiff in their best clothes, or a young couple just married, with not much money to spare. One of the first times I helped Sam in the studio there was a farm family, the wife maybe not much older than me but with three little ones already. We heard the jingling harness, saw the wagon stop, all of them wrapped in blankets that they carried inside to warm up a little, bringing a cold smell. One of the boys ran back to stroke the big horse's nose, and white clouds swirled round his head.

The farm wife had a freckled face, and while Sam was arranging the children she asked me would those freckles show, and could we fix the photograph so they didn't. Sam had already told me that he never did that kind of painting, but behind a screen in the corner there was a shelf with a brush and a little pot of powder, and I took her there, patted her cheeks and forehead while she closed her eyes. I undid her hair and did it up again, a little looser, and when she looked in the oval mirror, something in her face let go.

Those farm children were good as gold, young as they were, but there were always ones that couldn't sit still, or had a sudden need to stick a finger up their nose. I bought rock candy at Hatch's grocery, and a big glass jar to keep it in, and I told the children that if they didn't fidget, didn't move, they could have any piece that they wanted. I stood right beside Sam, holding the jar, and most of them never took their eyes off it. *You're a genius, Abby. You are,* Sam told me, and I walked home over the bridge that day feeling like one of those children, with sweetness dissolving on my tongue.

· · ·

The first time Sam took me into his dark-room it reminded me of things I don't like to think about and I had trouble with my breath, thought that I might suddenly scream or faint. I don't think Sam knew; he kept on talking in his teaching voice, and I held on to that. I watched him pouring, watched him gently rocking the dish from side to side, end to end, and my breathing eased, the pounding stopped. I found I could see, in the spooky red light, could hear the soft putter of the gas lamp, make out the words Sam was saying, and not just the sound of his voice. He was explaining about the dark, how important it was, and he told me a story he'd read about a woman somewhere in the West, who packed up two horses and went off for weeks at a time, photographing trees and mountains and wild rushing rivers. *A woman doing that,* he said. *And using wet collodion too.* I didn't know what that meant, but I guessed it was something that made her life harder. Sometimes, Sam said, this woman, whose name he'd forgotten, used her own black skirt as a dark-tent to develop her plates, all alone, up in the high mountains.

All the time Sam was telling me this I was watching his hands, rocking the tray, watching how the plate began to change. Parts of it turning black, but slowly, so slowly, and then other parts, lighter shapes, as if an invisible hand was drawing it, as if, somehow, it was drawing itself. I said something like that, and Sam smiled at me in the red glow, said, *I've done this hundreds of times, really hundreds, but I always think that too.*

. . .

When old Mr. Cowan died, he left me some money. Not a great deal of money, but enough for some people to say they'd been right all along. There was never any truth in it. He was a kind man, Mr. Cowan, and even at the end he thanked me for every bit of food I spooned into his mouth. I was sorry to leave my room with the flowered paper, bigger even than my room in the Doctor's house, but there was enough money to pay at Mrs. Bell's a few months in advance, enough that I could look for a different kind of work. I bought myself a new hat from Becks', with a brim that stood up on one side and a feathery plume, and I wore it for luck the day I walked over the footbridge. *To assist half-days,* the advertisement said, *in a busy photographer's studio. Must be of good character and tidy in personal habits.* No mention of the wage but I thought almost anything would do, for work that wasn't scrubbing and cooking and sweeping out grates.

The first thing Sam said when he opened the door was, *My, what a hat,* and then he walked me through the few rooms of the house, talking all the time. First the studio, with its jumble of chairs and a cloth screen painted with faraway hills. Shelves on one wall with photographs standing in frames and leather folders, though I didn't have time to see what they were. In the room he called the dark-room he took the black cloth off the small window and I saw a large stone sink and some kind of barrel, a workbench piled with trays and basins, with other things I still don't know the names of. A chest of drawers where he said he kept plates and papers, and more shelves on the wall, filled with brown bottles of different sizes, each one labeled with strange words. I would have to learn all this, Sam said, and he asked me if I liked to learn, and I said, *Yes sir.*

The other room he showed me was the kitchen, and that was in a terrible state. It had one tall window, looking out on the river, and the light that came through showed everything. Sticky stains on the floor and a table piled with books and papers, a heel of bread starting to color and rough crumbs lying everywhere. A knife with something smeared on the blade, and a pot of honey with hard tears dripped down the side. There was a door half open and through it I could see a rumpled bed, but Sam pulled it shut when he saw me noticing. *One thing*, Sam said. *I forgot to say in the advertisement, but can you read and write? Yes sir,* I said, and he picked up a limp-covered book from the table, shook the crumbs off and said, *Try this.* And I read: *There is nothing in the understanding that was not first in the sense.* And: *My life is wasted with heaviness, and my years with mourning.* Those words were harder and I stumbled a little, but Sam just said, *So you can.*

I might have told him, if he'd asked, that my brother Frank and I could both read, that we used to take turns with the green book we had, when our mother had trouble with the light. I might have told him about the classroom at Miss Weir's, and what happened when we made a blot on the page. But he didn't ask, just said could I start with a bit of a tidy, and I looked around and saw that I was not done with scrubbing after all.

. . .

Frank was the oldest, though I don't remember how old. Maybe eleven, maybe twelve. Too big to sleep in the bed with the rest of us, and for a long time he'd been out running messages, selling newspapers, doing other things too, I guess. The first time he came home with silver coins my mother slapped his face, but then she took them anyway, and then she cried. That was when we were all picking rags, ripping the seams of big bundles of shirts and coats and trousers and piling them in other big bundles. If there was no rain we could sit in the doorway, where the light was better. Frank left us slowly, started going out after my mother had gone, sometimes coming back just before she did in the dawn. Sometimes not at all, and then more and more nights like that, until we didn't see him for weeks at a time. He always brought a little money, when he did come, and a package with bread and other things, and he teased us all like he used to, and my mother watched him with a look on her face.

. . .

I can only know for sure about the ones who have children. Mrs. Bell, my landlady, who puffs her way up the stairs, and I picture her with Mr. Bell, the gray hairs that poke out of his nose, I can't help it. Mrs. Toller, so pale and whispery, who always greeted me kindly; I used to wonder if she saw the Reverend's face the way I've seen Sam's, wide open. All the women I see on the street, or in a shop; I look at them, but I can't imagine that it could be anything the same. Some days I am so full of Sam, so full of the two of us, that I can't even think; I hear my voice asking for a half pound of cheese in Hatch's, and it's as if it belongs to someone else, someone who's still just walking through their life. Someone as far away as the girl who used to cry, her head pushed down in the stinking straw.

And my mind is filled with the things I've learned, things I never thought to wonder about the world. When sunlight falls through the chip in the studio skylight, bands of color fall on the floor, climb a little way up the wall. Sam told me how the rough edge of the chip separated the colors so that we saw them, but they were there all the time, in the everyday light around us. Then he picked up the blue glass dish that held the river stone and the dried rose petals, emptied those things into his cupped hand and asked me did I know why the dish was blue. I didn't know what to say, but it didn't matter because Sam was already explaining. He said that when light fell on the dish some of the colors, those invisible colors that made up the light, were absorbed by it. Fell into it and were trapped there, forever. But the blue part of the light, for some reason that I forget, bounces back to our eyes and makes us think that the dish is the color we call blue. I looked around the studio, looked at all the colors there, the dull red settee and the cushion on the cane chair, the sky-blue shirt hanging on the doorknob and the rich leather folders on the shelf. And I thought about the light falling on all of them at the same time, but each thing being different in what it took into itself, in what it would not accept, but flung back at our eyes. There was a thought I almost caught hold of, but then Sam tipped everything back into the dish and it was gone. A stray petal drifted to the floor and was crushed beneath his boot as he walked away.

My head was filled with things I learned from Sam, but there was no one I could talk to about them except for Sam himself. I tried to tell Lucy, sitting with cups of tea like we sometimes did, in the Doctor's kitchen, in the quiet part of the afternoon. It was still strange to visit there, Mrs. Doctor asleep upstairs and the Doctor out on calls or closed in his office. Eaton at school now but signs of him everywhere, a muddy boot by the back door, the trousers Lucy was darning, that looked impossibly large. The same dishes in the rack, the green milk jug, the same life going on without me. I picked up that green jug and I explained to Lucy about the light, what Sam had told me, but she just said, *What does it matter? It's green because it is, because that's what we call it, what does it matter why?* And then she said, *Watch yourself, Abby. Don't do anything foolish.* And she looked me straight in the eye, so I couldn't look away. *It's not like that,* I said, but Lucy said, *It's always like that.* So I hadn't explained that well either, hadn't made her understand how it was with Sam and me, how different.

. . .

The first thing Sam taught me was to mix the hypo to pour into the fixing tray, and he wrote it out for me so I would learn the right bottles, and watched while I measured. *Hyposulphite 2 ounces, washing soda ¼ ounce, the same of salt, and 18 ounces of water from the barrel.* Sam said, *It's like a recipe. Like something you'd use to make a cake.* It isn't anything like how I make a cake, but it's not difficult and I like measuring with the special spoons or the little brass scales, I like reading the names written on the bottles I take down from the shelves, names I practice saying when I walk home over the bridge. *Hydroquinone, acetone sulphite, potassium carbonate*. The gloves make everything awkward and now my fingers are often stained black, like Sam's were, curled around the door he first opened to me. That's something else I learned from him, that our bodies are always changing. That new skin is always growing, that even stains the hardest scrubbing won't touch will eventually disappear.

Sam always talks when we're working together and sometimes he tells me things about when he was a boy, growing up in the next town. He had an older brother named Peter and a younger one named John and they were always in trouble, sneaking off to the river with their fishing poles instead of chopping wood or unloading sacks of grain from the wagons. Almost every day their father had to pick up the leather strap, bend them over his scarred oak desk, but Sam says that never made any difference. He asked me once if I had brothers and sisters, and I knew it would be easier if I said I didn't, but that seemed a terrible thing. So I told him I had four, and tried to think what I would say when he asked me more. But he didn't ask more, so I needn't have worried.

Sam's father was a grocer first, but then a photographer too, and even I had heard of him. When I worked in Dr. Robinson's house, Mrs. Doctor wanted a portrait taken, and of course no one in this town was good enough, only Joseph Ryan would do. That was some years ago and it's strange to think that maybe Sam was there too, adjusting a fold in Mrs. Doctor's dress, turning little Eaton's head this way and that. Sam and his father had some kind of falling out and he came to Emden to set up on his own; it's not so many miles but he says he hasn't been back, that there were too many harsh things said. His brother John runs the grocery now, and Peter is off in New York doing something, so he doesn't see them either. If I'd known him better when he told me all that I would have said something, would have made him see that a family's not a thing to be so lightly thrown away.

. . .

My sister Millie took it hardest, when our mother didn't come home and instead it was Miss Weir and a policeman taller than any man we'd ever seen. Miss Weir wrinkled her nose and kept her mouth shut, except to tell us that our mother had gone away and we were to come with her. Millie was sitting on the floor, holding the baby, and from where she was they must have looked like giants, blocking out the little bit of light from the door. She squeezed the baby so tight it began to wail, and that made Jim start too. But the policeman squatted down; he was still big, but not so enormous, and he chucked Jim under the chin and told him that if he stopped crying, he'd show him a bit of magic. Then he did something with his hand and pulled a peppermint from Jim's ear and gave it to him to suck, and that was the end of Jim's tears, and I suppose that was the moment he was lost to us. He was only little; he can't be blamed.

In the carriage Miss Weir put her face close to mine, her long teeth, and said, *Do you know how old you are, dear?* I was so astonished that I blurted out *Eight,* but when she asked if I knew my birthday I put my lips together, my head down. She asked Millie the same questions, but Millie understood, and didn't say a word. Jim didn't know, and the baby hadn't had a birthday yet. *Well then,* Miss Weir said, over the rattling wheels, *Let's say today is your birthday, all your birthdays, and when we get home we'll have cake to celebrate.* And we did have cake, in the room with the long tables, where the rows of children sat quietly. After we'd cleaned a plate with more food than we'd ever seen at one time. Millie and I were terribly sick in the night, and I worried about Jim, off in the boys' side, who must be sick too. And I worried about the baby, even though it didn't have cake, but we never saw the baby again.

· · ·

Sam's house had been a photographer's before, already had the skylight that brightens the front room studio and lets in drips when it rains. It belonged to a man named Simmons, a man no one knew much about, except that he had a scar on his cheek and a fine baritone voice for singing hymns. He was there for some years and then he wasn't, and when someone noticed that, no one could remember how long it had been.

The town clerk packed up some things he'd left behind and rented the house to Sam, saying they'd see, in a year or two. It was already longer than that and Simmons' things took up space Sam needed in the dark-room, so one afternoon when the rain drummed down he carried the boxes into the studio and I made a space between the bowls plinking with rainwater. There were bundles of small mounts for visiting cards, and one box inside a larger one was filled with ladies' caps and bonnets, some made of straw and some curled up on themselves like small dead animals. There were milk white plates, all prepared for the camera, and boxes of spoiled ones, some exposed, some not. A good black coat that looked like it might fit Sam, but he wouldn't try it on. One box had winter scenes, and some of them were of this house, with icicles hanging from the eaves. A few of the frozen river with no houses in sight, somewhere a cold walk away. Underneath those, wrapped in a red cloth, were five or six negative plates, ready to be printed, with dates marked in the corners like all the others. I turned them this way and that, but I couldn't make out what they were. Sam took one from me and held it up, turned it around, and then his cheeks went red, the tips of his ears. *I think,* he said, *I think they're his—private parts.* I stared at him while the idea worked into my understanding, and when it did it was so peculiar that I started to laugh, Sam did too, and we laughed until we had the worst pain.

Sometimes, in the house, I think of Mr. Simmons, and where he might be in the world. What it was that made him walk away, not caring who would find what he left behind. I imagine that he closed the door in early morning, when the mist sometimes curls and rises from the river; maybe he sang as he walked, but there was no one to hear his voice growing fainter and fainter. And I think that it's something like that, like a thick mist has swirled up and when it thins to nothing everyone is gone and I have no idea where they might be, how they will be living. Except for Miss Weir; she has disappeared too, I suppose, but I know where she will be, what she will be doing. I can picture her, standing straight in her dull brown dress, telling us to fold our hands and pray. Or leading some child away down the dim hall, with a firm grip on its ear. The head bent away and the feet scrabbling, trying to keep up to her swishing pace.

There was a painting in the room Miss Weir called her parlor, the room where she had her gleaming desk. A painting of a whiskery man, a hard-jawed woman, a little girl with ringlets, holding a doll and sitting on some kind of stool between them. *My parents,* she said, when she saw me looking, and that meant that she was the little girl with the full mouth, the rosy cheeks. I wondered, looking at that little girl, if she could ever have imagined that she would grow up to be Miss Weir, and I wondered what she thought about, all those hours sitting on that hard stool, trying to keep still, the yellow-haired doll smiling in her hands. Perhaps it was because of that I believed her, when she looked at me with her brown eyes and said that of course my mother knew, would be able to follow us later. When she told me that the crossing would be an adventure, that there was a wonderful new life waiting for us all. From the things Sam has told me I know that nothing in the world is just what it seems, that there are laws operating underneath, and hidden reasons. Even the purest-looking things, a scattering of sunlight, or the soft green of new leaves on the trees. But long before I met Sam, I knew I'd never believe anything so easily again.

• • •

I learned things faster than Sam thought I would, and more of them, and he was pleased with that because it gave him more time for the work he really wanted to do. The portraits he takes in the studio pay the rent of the house, pay for supplies, although it's always a struggle. But Sam doesn't want to be like his father, content with that. He's more interested in shadows and light, the shape of a rock rising out of the river, the splintered boards of a fence by the station. Last year Mr. Lett hired him to photograph all the buildings Mr. Marl owns in Emden, the businesses, the houses and the empty land. The photographs were presented to Mr. Marl on his birthday, and apparently he was very happy with them. Now Mr. Lett has given Sam another commission, hired him to take more photographs of the town that he will have made into a book. Mr. Lett says that he will give this book to men he knows of in the city, to help persuade them to build factories here, to give more money for his railway, money for other things. It seemed strange to me that anyone would do that for a place they've never been, but Sam said they would, if they thought it would bring them more money. He develops those photographs himself but shows me when they turn out like he wants. He's almost finished, and when Mr. Lett pays him we will be able to settle with Hatch, and maybe a few other places. If there's enough money, Sam wants to order some dry plates already prepared, from a place he's heard of in New York.

Mr Lett with his loud voice has come by once or twice, and he's pleased with what Sam's done, but also impatient. Some of the views I have trouble recognizing, even when Sam tells me. It looks like quite another town in his photographs, the buildings higher and the street in front of the shops bustling with people. Sam explained how he had placed the camera, the angles he used, and how one morning he gathered up every person who would come with him and put them in a group outside Linton's dry goods. It puzzled me, what he said, and I asked him how that was any different from covering up lines on a sitter's face, from coloring lips, or changing their shape to be more pleasing. Sam always says that's the wonder of photography, a record of the world just as it is instead of someone's idea of it, and I know that was one of the arguments he had with his father, things he was asked to do. *It's different,* he said, and he said that there was a purpose to these, that it was just a matter of showing what was already there, of showing it in the most appealing light. I still didn't see the difference, and I wanted him to explain so that I could understand, the way he's explained so many things. I didn't even realize I was making him cross until he said, *What would you know about it,* and walked away.

The next day I asked if I could come with him, when I saw him packing things ready. There was not much work to be done in the studio, and I said that I could help carry things, set them up, that I wanted to see how he did it. A beautiful day for the two of us to be walking across the footbridge together, and I remembered something Lucy had said. *Does he ever take you out?* she said. *To a concert at the church, or even for a Sunday walk? Ask yourself that,* Lucy said. But here we were, on a sunny morning, walking through town together for all to see.

It was market day, and Sam wanted to photograph the new shed, the bustle of wagons and animals and people in high spirits. We could hardly hear ourselves over the bellowing of the cattle, and I made Sam laugh, telling him the first time I was sent with a bucket to milk a cow. Never having seen one, except in the distance, from the railway train that brought us from the ship to Miss Weir's New Home. The cow was at the first place I was sent, and I had to leave Millie crying, climb up in the buggy with the sack that held my extra dress, some underthings, and a comb. They were not unkind to me there. I had my own bed, and the woman plaited my hair in the mornings. But I was no use to them at all on the farm and that was what mattered, nothing to do with how they might have liked me a little. When they brought me back to New Home I was full of things to tell Millie, but she was gone, and no one would tell me where. No one ever told me.

The place I was sent after that was not good, but the Doctor wrapped me in a blanket and took me home with him. Eaton was just a baby, and I knew quite a bit about babies, so that was all right. But sometimes in dreams even now I'm sitting in a room with Millie, and I wake up feeling so happy. On those days I think that I will somehow travel to New Home, that I will sit on the hard bench inside the front door and refuse to move until someone tells me where she went. If I'd told the Doctor, he might have done something, and I don't know what I was so afraid of then. If I told Sam, even all these years later, he would have a plan in a minute, and once or twice I've been on the edge of it. But he would wonder why I've waited so long, would maybe think me foolish, or hard. He wouldn't understand that there are worse things than not knowing.

. . .

People love to talk in this town and they have no trouble finding things to talk about; even the kindest seeming can be harsh judges. After the man Heath shot his family there was nothing else people wanted to hear about, everyone trying to find reasons. Women who had given me looks but never met my eye asked me things, because of living next door at Mr. Cowan's for a time, but I didn't have anything to tell, not really. Once I saw the older girl back by the raspberry canes with a knife in her hand but that wasn't anyone's business, and anyway they had plenty to talk about without it. Some said that Heath had stolen money from Mr. Marl, that it was something to do with the shame of that, and others said he was mad, or evil. The wildest stories floated around and maybe one of them was true or maybe none were, but I never did see that knowing a reason would make any difference. It was a terrible thing to happen, of course it was, a shocking thing. But hard things do happen every day to someone, things that are not at all their fault. You could spend your whole life wondering, and what good would that do? There are things even Sam, with all his Science, can't know.

. . .

Sam's hair is wild brown curls and it looks like he's been running his hands through it, even though he doesn't very often do that. Sometimes when he's trying to keep his temper, like with the lady in the big hat who brought her little dog, or sometimes when he's staring at the pictures he's taken for Mr. Lett, trying to decide which ones to show him. Once I cut Sam's hair, in the studio, under the skylight. The sun pouring through was warm on my face and hands, and he shuddered when the wet curls fell on his bare shoulders.

The first time I saw Sam angry was that day of the lady with the hat. After I cleaned up the mess the little dog left in the hallway I made us tea, but he couldn't sit still to drink it, pacing and talking but not really to me. Saying he'd had enough of it, enough of everything here. He still talks like that from time to time, says he'll write to his brother Peter, says New York is the place he should be. I try not to, but sometimes just before I fall asleep I picture the two of us in New York, on a street with tall buildings, crowds of people in fine clothes. I know what Lucy would say to that, know what she thinks, for she's told me often enough. I can't explain to her how I can believe and not believe at the same time.

· · ·

People come to the studio for different reasons, and sometimes I stand beside Sam and have the strangest thoughts. Looking at the young man holding a book just so, or the way the families are arranged, a baby on her mother's lap, a wife with her hand on her husband's shoulder, children placed according to height, and which ones can sit together without pinching. I stand beside Sam and I'm as invisible as he is, behind the tall camera, and I can look at them and know that they don't see me at all. Look at them and see not just what appears in the dark-room, what is inside the frame of the picture they will take home, but all the rest of it too. The flaking wall above the screen Mr. Simmons left behind, painted with pale hills and sky. A woman's toes tapping, just the toes of one foot, as if she can't keep everything in. The sisters who look straight at the camera, but reach for each other's hands.

Sometimes it's a couple just married, and they come with a few friends, family, who wander about the room. Stand behind Sam and pull faces, trying to make them laugh. Often they're all in a hurry because there's a train to catch and I wonder why they've made time for this, in the middle of their day, as if it's not complete unless they have something they can hold in their hands. I wonder if it will help them, years from now, to remember whatever it is they want to remember. How the wedding clothes felt against their skin, the scent from the lilac bush that leaned toward the front door. How they maybe felt that they could never be happier.

I think about the freckle-faced woman too, and why she minded so much. Maybe she was thinking of a time when she'd be gone, when her children would look at her photograph, hanging on a wall or standing on a table, and see those freckles and remember her, but not as she wanted them to remember. Her children growing older and everything fading; I know how that does happen. The smell of her, the sound of her voice, her hand on their hair. They'll look at her photograph and be left with a feeling, and be left with her freckled face. When they have their own children, those ones might remember a few stories they've been told, but for their children's children she'll be nothing but a name. They'll look at her picture and it won't remind them of anything at all, and maybe that's why it mattered.

Hers was the first plate Sam let me fix on my own, so perhaps that's why I often think of her. I thought there was something powerful in the hypo that would keep her face forever, but Sam said it wasn't that it kept things, but that it washed away all the extra salt that could spoil the plate later, left only what had been touched by the light.

Mornings the mist rises thick off the river, and sometimes when I put my foot on the steps beside the church I can't even see Sam's little house, on the other side of the bridge. Then I scare myself, thinking that it won't be there, that it will have vanished, or maybe never was. It's a nice kind of scaring, because underneath it I know that the house *will* be there, with the lean-to in back on the river side, the door that swells in the weather, and Sam maybe shut in the dark-room, or maybe just waiting for me.

Evenings when Sam has somewhere to be I go back to my room at Mrs. Bell's, sit and think about things while the sky goes mauve, then dark outside my window. I could never do what that mountain woman did, set off all alone and sleep by a fire at night, by the horses' shifting feet. I wouldn't know where to begin, standing in a grove of trees or by the side of a roaring river. But sometimes in town I see people, or find them stuck in my mind. The little boy who sells newspapers outside Malley's, or Mrs. Toller with her lost look, staring at the necklaces in the new jeweler's window. Old Mrs. Hatch in her rocker, with all the lines on her face. Sometimes I see people like that and wish that I had a hand camera, like the new one Sam bought, wish that I could catch them, at just that moment. I might even ask Sam, when Mr. Lett pays for the book and he's not so worried about money. I don't know what I would do with pictures like that, if I did find a way to take them. I'd like to borrow Mr. Bell's hammer and nail them up all over the wall of my room, but I don't suppose Mrs. Bell would allow that. Or maybe just keep them all together in one of the boxes we emptied of Mr. Simmons' things, that day we laughed and laughed.

There was one photograph in with all Mr. Simmons' spoiled plates, and I kept it out when we sealed everything up again. It was larger, mounted on stiff gray card, with a title in black ink, barely faded, each letter beautifully drawn. The title was *Market Day,* and I thought it must be a joke, although it seemed an odd one. The photograph showed the street by the wide square where the market is held, long before the shed was built. The oak trees there, but so much smaller. It was taken from a bit of a distance, but you could see wagons standing and a few long tables piled with something, one old horse with its head drooping. But there was not a person to be seen, and that was why I thought it was a joke, thought that maybe Mr. Simmons had done something like Sam had, outside Linton's, that he had gathered up all the farmers and their wives, all the townsfolk walking down the street or bustling about the wagons, squeezing vegetables and arguing about the price. All the children chasing each other and getting in everyone's way. I thought that maybe Mr. Simmons had persuaded all the people to stand behind him, that they were there in a dark mass, shifting their feet and watching while he took the picture, impatient to get back to their business.

I asked Sam and he took the photograph from my hand, looked at the date written in the corner, and told me to look again. *Here,* he pointed. *And here.* There were things that I had thought were shadows, or maybe flaws in the plate or the bath, and Sam said perhaps some were that. But he told me that a picture taken that long ago, before modern processes, would have needed a very long exposure, that Mr. Simmons probably stood in his place for five minutes at a time, maybe longer. And because of that, anyone who was moving, anyone walking or bending again and again, anyone driving a wagon down the center of the road, would not be captured, would leave only a faint shadow, a ghostly trace of themselves. Sam said he could tell because there was nothing to cast those smudges, if they were real shadows, not in the places they were. He said that the old horse was probably asleep and that's why we saw it, and he said that there were probably others, other people who had been moving more quickly and left no mark at all.

. . .

It's very important to keep down the dust, and every day I go over the studio. Beat the mats outside if I can, and run a damp cloth over the big urn that has to be turned so the chip won't show, the little tables and the pedestals, the shelves where we display the photographs Sam says are the best. They used to be mostly outside pictures, the ones he said he got just right. The light, the developing, what he calls the *composition*. But I thought it would be better to have people, since that's mostly what he does here, that's the work that he depends on. Now we have families marching along the shelves, and the beautiful girl with the necklace, slightly larger, so she's what people see first. I know who that girl is, saw her looking at the house one day when I was shaking out a mat, but she didn't come in.

There's a screen in one corner of the studio, with a mirror on the wall behind it, and sometimes when I'm wiping it off I stop and look at myself, wonder if it's my mother's face I see. I'm not that many years younger than she was when we were taken and that's a strange thought, and it makes me wonder if I'm somehow living her different life. She used to tell us that things could always be worse, but to remember that they could get better too.

Back home there was a tin box, scratched and dented in one corner, hard to open. My mother kept it under the bed and inside was a jet brooch and a folded piece of paper that she said came from a Bible. On that paper were names, going back and back and back. Some of them so faint that even on the brightest day they were hard to make out, and some almost worn away where the paper was folded. But my mother knew them all, and sometimes she would recite them all. Andrew and Christopher and Francis and Edward, Winnie and Beatrice and Thomas. Florence and Abigail and Mercy and Patrick, and on and on. *These are your people,* my mother used to tell us, *and you should always remember their names.* It was my fault, but there was no time to think when Miss Weir and the tall policeman stood in our doorway, blotting out the sun. In what seemed like an instant we were rattling away out of our life and I should have been quick enough; I should have thought to grab that tin box, to somehow bring it with us. But I wasn't quick, didn't even remember it until later, lying in the dark, and by then it was much too late.

It's not so sharp now, but I still don't like to think of my mother picking her way down the narrow lane. Coming back to our room, whenever she did, and finding other people there. Other people sleeping in our bed, sitting on our chair. Using the tin box themselves, or maybe they had sold it on. I don't like to think of her trying to find us everywhere, and no one telling her a thing. What I hope is that some little bit of good came from it, that maybe her life isn't so hard, with only herself to take care of.

I used to wish I had a photograph to carry with me, to stand up on the table beside my bed. One of all of us together, and I used to think that if only I had that it would be a comfort, and their faces wouldn't have faded. Now I'm not so sure. The photograph Mrs. Doctor had taken showed all three, with Eaton sitting so close between them, and it gives no idea of how they lived in their separate rooms. When we came to Miss Weir's she burned all our clothes, told us she did, and it's true they were ragged things, and not too clean. If I had a photograph I would see that, and maybe remember how cold my feet always were, the times the little ones cried. I would see Jim's crooked eye and remember that instead of Jim himself, and how we all were together.

·   ·   ·

Sam always finds it strange when we show someone their mounted photograph and they say, *Why, it looks just like me.* He mimics them later, and says, *Of course it looks just like them, what do they think? What do they think the camera does?* But I don't think that's exactly what they mean. The full red lips of the little girl who was Miss Weir, in the painting, would never have been hers in life. Sam's father might have done that same thing in a photograph, the way he made the sad lines on Mrs. Doctor's face disappear, but even though Sam wouldn't, it seems to me that the pictures I wrap up for the sitters show them an idea of themselves that pleases, and he is part of that. How he arranges them, the things he has them hold, or places in the background. Sam's pictures show them in their best clothes, in light that is the most flattering, close to the people who matter to them. The ones who are not happy, who refuse to pay and say that they knew all along that they should have gone to Taylor, or McKim, they must see something that's not the way they want to think of it, something that doesn't fit. That's what I think, but it's hard to say in words. When I tried to tell Sam he listened, but his fingers were fiddling with the buttons on his vest.

. . .

It doesn't happen so often now, but there have always been nights when I wake up already frightened. Afraid to sit up, to move at all, afraid to go to the dark window. I have to make my breath come deep and slow so that I can stop the pounding in my ears, so that I can hear whatever there may be to hear. A lonely dog barking or a bit of a song from someone stumbling home. Mrs. Bell snorting in her sleep, in her room down the hall. I lie very still until I hear a sound that tells me that I'm not left alone in the world, that I'm not the last thing alive in the world.

If there's a high moon on those nights it slips through the gap in my curtains and makes a cold pattern on the wall by my bed. I try to stare at that, just stare at that, and not let the night thoughts in. Things I should have known, or done. I stare at the light and the dark and try not to see Sam settling a hat on his curly head, closing the door like Mr. Simmons, and walking away from everything. Mr. Cowan told me once that all night thoughts are different from day ones, that everyone knows what it is to be afraid, what it is to have doubts in the dark. One of those nights I sat in the chair by his bed while he waited for the powders to work. He liked the lamp kept low, and it was easier not to see the bones beneath his thin skin. He used to say that he'd seen enough, that the world was changing too fast, all the new ideas and discoveries. And he used to say that once a thing has happened, there is no going back. Sam says things like that too, but not in a sad way.

If everyone lies awake in the dark, like Mr. Cowan said, then the mountain woman did too, and I wonder what she told herself, so that she could close her eyes again. It must have been that the plates she packed away so carefully were worth all the trouble she took. And even Miss Weir, in her hard narrow bed, must have wondered, must have had to believe it was all for the best. Sometimes I see Eaton running with his friends, or rolling a hoop in the dusty street and I think that he's not so much older than I was; he's just a boy and I wouldn't expect him to save anyone.

I wonder too if there was a boy like Eaton, rolling his hoop through the market the day Mr. Simmons took his photograph. Maybe he's one of those smudges, or maybe there were several boys, girls too, running like children do. Moving so fast they left no trace at all, free to run on into any kind of life.

KNIFE

MR. LETT DIDN'T find it, although he prowled through
the house, every room, before the windows were boarded
up. Looking for answers, looking for an explanation he could
present to the old man, who was gnawing at the thing as if it was
something personal. Unlike him to be so rattled, and unlike him
to have been fooled, if that's how it was. How often had Marl
said, snipping a fine cigar or capping his gold pen with a snap,
how often had Lett heard him say, *I didn't get where I am without knowing what makes a man tick*. Tempting to see it as the first
sign of decline, raging about the embezzlement and then sending Lett with the bail —what kind of sense did that make?
Good money wasted on inquiries that went nowhere, and then
on a lawyer who couldn't possibly make any difference. It was
tempting to hope that the long waiting was nearly done, but Lett
knew that kind of thinking was dangerous, that he would have
to be even more careful, not let the faintest glimmer show. He

knew how those sleepy, hooded eyes could flash fire, could burn a man up when he least expected it. So he reined in his thoughts and his boots were loud and slow in the rooms of the house, his pen scratching in the little notebook as he entered his estimates of the value of things. Not much, and not much to see either. Dishes on the table, a newspaper, a jacket hanging on a hook. Stains on the floors that would have to be scrubbed out, but other than that it was just a house that a family had lived in, the things they had left behind not worth anything at all.

Mr. Lett didn't find it, but Bash did, after the trial. In the house with two others to cart things away for the sale. It fell out from under a mattress, a folding knife with a yellowed bone handle, the tip broken off but the blade sharp, so sharp that his testing touch drew a thin line of blood that welled and darkened. Someone else might have wondered what it was doing there, might have called to the others, passed it around, and talk might have flickered through the town. But Bash just slipped it into his pocket, blotted his finger on the seam of his trousers and bent to heave the mattress again, last night's drink pounding in his head. Someone else might have settled at his kitchen table that evening, with a rag and a tin of polish. Might have noticed the stamped symbol on the blade, the heart and pistol, and marveled at it, another story passed around. But Bash just thought that he'd needed a knife and he'd found a knife, and that was the way things should work. A drop from his bleeding finger had fallen on a smooth black pebble that lay on the floor beside the bed; as he bent to the mattress, the toe of his boot sent it skittering into a dark corner, but he didn't notice that either.

EATON, LATER

And all the lives we ever lived and all the lives to be
Are full of trees and changing leaves . . .

—*Charles Isaac Elton*

FOR THE REST of his life he saw the hanging man in dreams and after Jenny died, when it seemed he had nothing left but time, he wondered if knowing that would have changed anything. Wondered if he would have closed his eyes again, burrowed back into sleep, not heard a sound until Lucy called his name from the doorway. Just like any other day.

It was a flicker of a question, not difficult to answer, even if he hadn't raised sons of his own. A boy of eleven didn't imagine a seamed face looking back from the mirror. Would never think of himself as an old man in a chair in a room, waiting for the sound of a key in the door, brisk footsteps. Waiting for someone who cared, but only a little, that he'd lived to see another blue day.

Those years when his days were busy and too short he'd often thought that all he lacked was a little empty time. Time to sit in the comfortable armchair, time to read, time to tease out those thoughts that rippled and sank again while he was doing other things. Who had said, *Be careful what you wish for?* Something he'd known once, but it was like those memories that were so familiar that his mind skidded off them, didn't let them play themselves out, for years and years. And then all at once they were gone, just fragments left, an outline, as if he had killed them through neglect. Like a flower in a garden, or maybe more like the silver frames Jenny stopped polishing. The filigree darkening, the picture inside fading, losing something it once had, when the frame was carefully tended and enclosed it.

If he hadn't seen the hanging that day, he knew that his life would have been different. Not necessarily better or worse, but different. The same way it would have been different if they'd stayed on in Emden after his father died, different if his father hadn't died. His mother always said that the Doctor was so busy taking care of other people that he neglected himself, simply left it too late. But when he was older, Eaton wondered. He had no memory of the process, although he must have seen the bandaged hand, must have seen something. They would have spoken to each other, eaten meals together, passed each other in doorways. He was there, right there; his father was dying on his feet while he was flicking marbles through a circle drawn in the dirt, while he was doing his lessons and thinking his thoughts and running through the wide fields at the edge of town.

He didn't think he'd really seen it, but he could picture his father sitting at the desk in his little office at the back of the house, staring at the gash across his palm. It happened quickly but that still meant days and he imagined the rolled sleeve, the red trails creeping up the arm. He came to believe that in the end it was a kind of suicide, that his father just watched, letting something else decide if he would live or die. He tried to ask his mother once, after a meal in a hotel, while they waited for his stepfather to fetch the car. But his mother said that was a wicked thing to even think, batted her hands as if he was still a pestering boy. She walked away from him, pushing open the heavy door to stand in the cold dark, and he followed her, cupped her sharp elbow in his hand as he helped her to the curb.

. . .

Even standing up required thought now and he kept a pile of books on the table beside his chair, tried to have something that would suit any mood. A comic novel his daughter had sent, a volume of Tennyson, a history of ancient Rome. His father's well-thumbed Burton was there too, and whenever he opened it, he found something that spoke to him. *Idleness of the mind is much worse than this of the body, maximum animi nocumentum.* On many pages there were passages, phrases that his father must have marked, faint pencil ticks in the margins. There was a time when he had seen them as clues, remembered the way messages were passed on in the dime novels he had read as a boy and tried to string the ticked passages together into some kind of story or revelation. *Shame and disgrace cause most violent passions, and bitter pangs.* It had been important once, and then at some time it had stopped being important. Now even his youngest son was years older than his father had been when he died.

There were also a few mystery novels on the table, the kind of titles he used to tease Jenny about. *Sparkling Cyanide, The Bride of Death, Evil Under the Sun.* Jenny was the most even-tempered person he had ever known and possibly the kindest, but she loved to read about murder and mayhem, bloody crimes committed with stilettos and blunt instruments. After she left he picked up the book on her night table, wiped off the thin film of dust before he opened it. Now the woman next door brought him several each week from the library, and he understood what he hadn't bothered to before. The appeal of chaos, always followed by order restored, the different ways the same pattern worked itself out each time.

Jenny had left behind notes too, shopping lists and little reminders to herself. It had been a family joke for years, how she made lists of everything, and weeks after she was gone he was still finding them, scribbled on bits of paper, on napkins folded in the pockets of coats and dresses, inside the flour canister. Clues to herself that wrenched his heart: *milk-cold-white. Ellie long dark hair.* He thought of how frightened she must have been, and how she had never said. Or maybe she had; that was worse. Maybe he had been so caught up in doctors and appointments and prescriptions that he hadn't let himself hear it.

It was very cold the day Jenny left her life, the wheels of the ambulance crunching along their snow-covered street. Blue light of early morning. The men were as gentle as their voices, but the rattle of the wheeled stretcher scraped the air raw. She couldn't speak but her eyes told him that she knew, as surely as a condemned criminal, that this was the last trip down the green carpeted stairs, straps drawn tight over the red blanket. Knew that this cold on her face was the last real air she would feel. The winter sky was webbed with trees, wisps of smoke rising, the snow-covered peaks of houses, and he knew that she was filling her eyes with the last of the world.

Later he imagined that she had closed her eyes when the ambulance doors clicked shut, but at the time his mind was swept bare, only able to notice small, discrete things. The tremor in his hand as he turned the key in the lock, the cold plastic smell inside his car. A light flicking on in a house as he turned a corner and the way the big car seemed to glide through the dead gray streets, his own pale hands on the steering wheel. Jenny lingered another whole day, enough time for their children to arrive and stroke her forehead, hold her hands, but she didn't look at anyone again. Sitting in the hard chair beside the hospital bed, he knew that what he was feeling was the rest of his life without her.

．　．　．

He didn't know that he dreamed much anymore, sleep now a state he floated in and out of through the long nights, the longer days. He had promised his children that when the stairs became too much he would sell the house but they didn't need to know, no one did, the way he lowered himself so carefully, using his cane and the polished railing, the way he bumped himself down like a small child would, the red and gold light falling through the transom onto the carpet in the front hall, so far below. Some days were harder and he had to rest a little, halfway up or down, listening to the creaking house, sometimes a car going by, voices from the street. It reminded him of something, but these days everything reminded him of something else. As if he'd lived so long that nothing was new, as if he could only go back and around again, everything a strange echo of a pattern already laid down. He wasn't sure when it had started to feel that way. The day he and Jenny had first looked at the house they had stood in the hallway, the same rosy light touching Jenny's hand where it lay on his sleeve. *It's perfect,* she said. *Don't you think it's the perfect house for us?* And he had agreed, pushing down the vague uneasiness he felt, something to think about some other time.

He didn't think he dreamed much now, but when he did it was the same. Any kind of dream: an empty street or children splashing at the seaside, Eaton himself riding a bicycle on a sunny day, feeling the breeze in his hair. At some point he would turn a corner, would turn around, and the hanging man would be there. Sometimes everything pulsed with a rasping sound, sometimes just the black comma shape, swaying a little at the end of a thick rope. And always the dream-thought: *Of course*. The dream-knowledge that the hanging man was always part of the story, that Eaton had been foolish and forgotten, that the ticking shape would always appear, at some point, and change whatever was unfolding into something else.

It didn't terrify him as it had when he was a boy, those nights he still remembered when he fought to stay awake as long as he could, when he chanted prayer after prayer, trying to seal every gap in his mind. All that came rushing back when his own children were growing, calling out in the night. He remembered settling the covers around Ellie, smoothing her hair and saying, *It was only a dream*. Something about claws, and water dripping on stone. Ellie's eyes popped open again and she said, *But what if **this** is the dream? This part right now?* He wanted to tell Jenny, when he finally slid back into their soft bed, but she was far away, breathing deeply. Leaving him alone in the dark, alone with the strange thought: *Do I dream the hanging man, or does he dream me?*

• • •

The woman who came every few days to tidy things had faded blond hair in tight curls and a large wild family. Her name was Brenda and she was always in a hurry, crashes in the kitchen and a simultaneous shout of *Botheration!* Things that had survived years of washing and drying and growing children rattled in pieces as she tipped them from the dustpan, but he didn't really care, and when the heavy vacuum was back in its place, the last counter wiped and her apron on its hook behind the door, they always drank a cup of coffee together. These days Brenda and the grocery boy were the only people he could count on seeing, and when she'd bustled out the back door he sat back in his armchair, reclaimed the quiet house, now smelling of polish and bleach and a casserole warming in the oven. With his eyes closed he was reminded of the kitchen of the house in Emden, Lucy's cracked red hands gentle on his face.

He'd tried from time to time but he didn't remember anything about leaving Emden, the good-byes he must have said, promises made. The closest he could come was sitting up in the dark wooden bed in his grandfather's house, all the city noises through the open window although it was long after dark. On his pulled-up knees he held the one Drifter Dan story his mother had allowed him to bring, and he remembered bending his head until his nose touched the thin paper, breathing in as deeply as he could, a faint whiff of something that made his heart sore. There was an idea in his head about running away, but his grandfather's house was in the center of the sprawling city and he was too tired to even begin to think about the plan he would have to make. Instead, he decided that he would bide his time, pretend to get used to the new boots and the streetcars, the visits to the museum and the long staircases in the crowded school. He supposed that while he was pretending he did get used to it, and that became his life.

· · ·

After Jenny died he wanted to do it all himself but his children thought that it would be a good opportunity to clear out other things too, and they all stayed over for a few days, sleeping in their old rooms, making meals and washing dishes and wearing him out with their laughter and their memories. The things they exclaimed over—a souvenir milk jug, shaped like a black and white cow, the old button jar, a battered lampshade with beaded fringe. Things he'd had no idea meant anything to anyone.

From the back of the cupboard under the stairs one of them pulled out a box that Eaton's stepfather must have passed on. Brittle letters that his mother had kept, some written in his own hand. A heavy desk clock with a cracked face, and a mounted photograph, freckled with age. The photograph reappeared beneath the next Christmas tree, cleaned up and framed under glass, and he held it in his hands in the pine-scented room, doing his best to pretend that it mattered much more than it actually did. The name *Ryan* was written across one corner, touched up in gilt script. Eaton a round-cheeked boy of five or six, with a wary look in his eyes. He sat between his mother and his father, some kind of blurry backdrop behind them. His mother was beautiful in her high-necked dress, and his father's mustache was thick and dark. At the bottom of the photograph part of Eaton's left hand was visible; it must have been resting on his father's leg, and although the frame cut most of it off he could still see the curve of his father's knuckles, knew that cupped hand covered his own.

That Christmas morning they stood the framed photograph on the mantelpiece, and his grandchildren squealed as they ripped at brightly colored paper and stuck silver bows in their hair. A few times he realized that he was looking to meet Jenny's eyes, knew that time had briefly collapsed, generations confused, the same rituals in the same room. Jenny would have understood about the gift, and if she hadn't, he would have been able to tell her. The rush of love he had felt for his children, who had thought of it, taken time and trouble. The pang that came too, the feeling that he had failed in some way, because the actual thing didn't mean what they had thought it would. He'd always known the photograph was somewhere in the house, meant to look for it, but not in any urgent way. He remembered it well, thought he did, and his children couldn't have known what he had felt, that earlier day when they dragged out the dusty box in the house still vast with Jenny's absence. Leaning over him, touching his shoulders when he held the thick, spotted cardboard in his hands. He'd felt nothing, that was the thing, the picture itself not much like his memory of it, not how he had thought of it, those times it slid into his mind. The thing he held in his hands was a photograph of three people in darkish clothes, sitting close together, with the hazy shapes of trees showing in the small spaces between them. Nothing more than that.

· · ·

At his retirement dinner Jenny sat across from him in a new green dress, earrings that caught the light. There were speeches and handshakes and funny stories from former students, catchphrases repeated to laughter and nods of recognition, although he'd had no idea that he was known for them. There were serious notes too, men in suits with Brylcreemed hair telling how Mr. Robinson had inspired them, how he had turned their lives around. Eaton put his hand over his glass when the waiter came around; he thought he must be a little fuddled by drink, listening to the speakers and wondering who they were talking about.

His own speech was short, and he hoped gracious, and he joked about writing his memoirs with the engraved gold pen, as if his days would suddenly become just time that needed to be filled. He even thought about it one rainy afternoon, thought about leaving a record for his children, something they would one day be glad to have. He supposed they would, but he also

remembered teenaged eye-rolling at the dinner table, looks exchanged in the backseat of the car whenever he said, *Did I ever
tell you about. . .* He remembered too the way he usually carried on anyway, the sound of the story, of his own voice telling it,
somehow more important than the fact that no one wanted to
hear it, that no one was even listening.

Instead of a memoir, he thought of working out a family
tree, thought of all the names, the straight lines drawn on thick
vellum paper. He had his mother's Bible somewhere, the pages
at the front covered in faded spiked or flowing script that could
be deciphered with strong light and a magnifying glass, now
that he had time. But he realized that his father's side was a mystery, wondered if it was possible that he had simply forgotten so
much. He tried to lean back into his mother's stories, anything
she might have said, but could find nothing before the one about
the day they had met, sitting on spindly chairs in a stuffy room
while a woman folded her hands and sang. He had the idea that
there was a farm involved somewhere, and a hard father or
uncle, but that was all and even if his mother was still alive he
wasn't sure that she would have told him more. For all that she
chattered there were so many things that his mother wouldn't
say, things that disappeared with her, although he supposed that
was true of everyone. Once, standing in a doorway, he heard her
say, *Emden—how I hated that place,* and the sentence made sudden sense of the way she'd changed.

· · ·

It seemed that Jenny had kept everything, every stick-figure
drawing, every smudged card, every tissue and pipe-cleaner
flower. Stacks of letters tied with different colored ribbons. Even
his sons were moved, going through the heavy bottom drawer,

and like his daughter they both made piles to take away with them. He wondered if that was the way it always happened, if there always came a time when you took back the gifts you had given, or when they were returned to you. And he thought then of Rachel's book, a thing he had always kept on his shelves, had never, for some reason, packed away to make space for other things. She had said it was a present for her family, asked him if he would keep it for her, just keep it until Christmas, because there was nowhere to hide things in her own house and she didn't want the surprise spoiled. And he didn't think anything of it, that day outside his house when she put it in his hands. A homemade book, not too big, not too heavy, the covers stiff and wrapped with glued-down cloth. He was worried about being late for supper, he remembered that, worried about making his mother cross, and he hurried inside, shoved it into a space on the small shelf in his room, beside the torn spine of *Mark Seaworth*. He didn't think anything of it until after she was dead, until he realized that he couldn't give it back, that there was no one left to give it to and it was all up to him, whatever would happen to Rachel's book. Plans chased around in his head. He thought of throwing it into the swirling river, of making a fire, of burying it in the heart of Jackson's wood. He thought of being its uneasy keeper for the rest of his life.

He hadn't even looked at the book until after the murders, opening it then in hope of finding a hint, some mention of a scar-faced stranger that would prove that everyone had it wrong. But there was nothing like that. He thought Rachel had said it was instead of a photograph that hadn't been taken, or hadn't come out well, but he didn't remember exactly or know if that was important. The front page of the book said *The Story of the Wonderful Whippets* in elegant lettering, and the following ones were drawings, some pen and ink, some brushed with paints, most also with writing in Rachel's neat hand. He looked through the book carefully, every page, but if there were clues he wasn't clever enough to find them.

Rachel's book had been somewhere on a shelf in every place he had ever lived, but it wasn't something he often thought about. Maybe only when he actually touched it, moving house or packing up boxes so a bookcase could be painted. Years apart, and he was older each time, seeing it differently. Seeing that the drawings, while very good, were still those of a child and not the marvels he had once thought. Noticing places where a word or phrase had been corrected, a piece of matching paper carefully cut and glued down, written over, obvious now that the glue had aged and dried, edges beginning to lift and curl.

And each time too there was the nagging question: why had she given it to him? Why really? Every house was filled with its own hiding places, something he wouldn't have thought of at the time. The same way he hadn't wondered why she had given it to him and not to someone like Miss Alice, why not to Miss Alice? Rachel was someone he knew for a few years when he was a boy, someone he might have played games with, might have talked with about the kind of things that children do. He didn't remember any closer connection, thought she would probably have disappeared completely from his memory if she hadn't died, hadn't died in that way. Like others in the town, others around Miss Alice's school table. Presences he felt, when he tried to reach back, but could no longer give a name or face.

Jenny had asked him about the book once, carried it into the kitchen where he was tinkering with a leaky tap. She knew that he'd seen an execution when he was a boy, and he had probably told her that it was a man who had murdered his family, no more than that. But for some reason, with Jenny standing near him in her flowered apron and the steady drip of water on a summer afternoon, he found himself saying more. He started telling her and the words kept coming, so many words, as if it was a story he'd often told himself, beginning to end, although he never had. The open books on the schoolroom table and the terrible weight of the short white coffin, the green of the leaves in the tree and the jerking legs, the black hood sucking in and out. Jenny said, *You poor thing,* and he started to say, *Not me, it wasn't about me,* but he realized that it probably was. Wasn't everything, in the end?

Jenny listened, and there were creases between her beautiful eyebrows. *As if she knew, isn't it,* she said. *A premonition. Or maybe not exactly that, but who knows what goes on behind a closed door? It came out of the blue for all of you in the town, but who knows?*

The tap dripped steadily behind them. Jenny touched his cheek with a hand that smelled very faintly of polish, of things clean and shining. *And she knew you would take care of it, didn't she,* she said. *Even then there was something about you, something that made her choose you.* Thinking of that now, of his own arms wrapping around her, he missed Jenny so much he didn't think he could bear it.

· · ·

When his mother married Mr. Parks, Eaton didn't think much about it, beyond the fact that they seemed well suited. So much had already changed, many things easier between the two of them, and when she spoke of his father, as she sometimes did, it was without the jaggedness around the words, around his name. Partly the way he heard it, as he grew older and farther away, but not just that. Once she even told a story about a man with a boil in an embarrassing place, another about a woman who sang hymns all the time his father was examining her. Things they had laughed about together, long before Eaton was born. It had opened something up, to know that there had been laughter, freed something in his memory of Emden and all that went with it that had always been wrapped, until then, by the way she had set it so firmly behind them. The only mention coming sometimes when she read out an item from the newspaper, tutted and said, *Just like that horrible man Heath.*

He didn't remember actually leaving Emden, but he was sure that he hadn't thought it would be forever. Even with his mother's aversion he might have kept some connection if it was closer to the city, or on the way to some other place they visited. That time might have stayed a part of his life instead of being sealed away by itself, something that would have taken a special effort to pierce. But as things were it took years and then one day, driving himself somewhere to give a speech or attend a meeting, he saw a sign and turned off the main road, followed a narrower secondary road he hadn't ever been on. Passing through small corner places he'd never heard of, thinking how strange it was that this was the way in, this was the way people came to Emden, this the countryside that had always enclosed it.

In town he came upon his own house quite suddenly, just as he was trying to remember how to find it. There was a small sign outside, a different doctor's name, but he thought that otherwise it probably looked much the same. People always said that things from their childhood looked so much smaller, when they saw them again, but that wasn't exactly what he noticed. What struck him instead, as he sat in the car, was how close together everything was. No distance at all between the market square he had driven through and his old house, the Barnes' next door where he went to school and the river that had seemed such a journey to reach, the line of trees that marked the start of the wood. All the parts of his life, the whole wide world he had lived in—on this blue day he felt he could almost take it in with the span of his arms.

From where he had stopped the car he could also see most of Will's house, the gloomy red brick, maybe even the same dull green door. For some reason he thought of Ophelia, a painting of Ophelia, floating with sodden flowers, and he tried to puzzle it out. Will's mother, that must have been the connection, although she hadn't drowned herself. An overdose of laudanum, maybe an accident, something he hadn't realized that he knew. He thought of the painting and something shivered as he understood that he must have seen Mrs. Toller in her coffin, must have seen her floating on the satin lining, flowers clutched in her dead hands.

The sky had darkened but no lights showed in Will's old house, no lights, he realized, in any of the houses around him. The entire landscape of his childhood seemed to be uninhabited, the only sound a tree branch somewhere, creaking in the wind. He had imagined himself strolling along the main street, maybe sitting down for a cup of coffee, even running into someone who remembered him, anyone at all. There had been a hazy idea that he would run into someone on the main street who would tell him the rest of the story, how things had turned out for everyone he had known, but suddenly that was the last thing he wanted. There was the sound of a door closing, and a gray-haired woman turned from the Barnes' front door, tucking a furled umbrella under her arm. He wondered if it could possibly be Miss Alice, and he thought that he could get out of the car, walk over and introduce himself; he thought what a wonderful thing it would be to see recognition come into her eyes. But even as the thought came he was turning the key, releasing the brake, the figure shrinking behind him as he pressed harder on the gas, no real thought again until he was back on the main road.

It couldn't have been the same day, but he wondered if his brief visit to Emden was connected to another memory, one that was so enclosed, so without any kind of context, that it might even have been a memory of a dream. He was in a car again, maybe the same car, driving through open country on a day filled with misty rain that wasn't really falling, but still saturated the air. He was in a car, driving through a pale, sodden day, and he was suddenly overwhelmed. Eased the car onto the shoulder, pulled the brake, opened the door, all those sounds registering, but without meaning. Then he was walking through long grass, the air around him filled with more water than it could possibly contain. He stopped in the misty field, his eyes on the far-off, hooded trees, and he felt as if he was trying to fill himself up, to somehow fill himself up through his eyes, through all his senses. It might have been a very long time that he stood like that, long minutes before he noticed that his eyelashes were beaded with water, before he became aware of his soaking feet, the unpleasant feeling of wet cloth wrapping his shins. He wasn't quite released, had to make himself turn, his feet slow at first, carrying him back toward the glistening black hump of the car at the roadside, the pale shapes that were the worried faces of his family, pressed against all the windows.

That was where it ended, this memory that might have been a dream. He believed it real only because it was so quiet, so complete, and because it brought with it a feeling of great peace, everything simply what it was and nothing at all lurking just out of sight.

. . .

Brenda came every few days and moved noisily through the house, crashes and bangs and the clatter of broken crockery. She vacuumed and dusted and left casseroles in the oven, did his laundry once a week and he had long since gotten over being embarrassed by things she might see. Before she left she carried in mugs of coffee, sat down in the other armchair with a great sigh. Sometimes they talked about the world but more often her no-good husband, her sons and nephews who weren't angels, she'd be the first to say, but not guilty of half the things they were blamed for. He told her about a friend he'd had once, said that although he had no idea how things turned out, he always pictured him on a cantering horse, mountains behind and an oiled rope coiled over the saddle horn.

Sometimes, of course, Brenda's boys really had done the things they were blamed for. Nothing too serious yet, but she worried all the time about where they were headed. Every day more sullenness, more swagger, their good hearts harder to find. *But they're mine, Mr. R,* Brenda always said. *I wouldn't change them for anything, not even if I could.* Eaton thought about that, and thought about how it was the kind of remark that might once have slipped into his ears and right out again, only a little niggle as it passed. Something like the pang he used to feel, watching his young sons swing from branches in the backyard, a feeling he thought he'd try to pin down one day, but now that there was time, nothing but time, he was no closer to under-standing. No closer to really knowing why he needed to puzzle over it. He only knew that he kept drifting back to Emden, as if there was something there, something that he couldn't really have forgotten.

Now that his children had grown into their lives, their own children too, there was no one who needed more than the idea of him, and he thought maybe that was why he had this nagging feeling, this sense that there were things he had to know for himself, only for himself. He knew, of course he knew, that a life wasn't anything like one of those novels Jenny read, that it stumbled along, bouncing off one thing, then another, until it just stopped, nothing wrapped up neatly. He remembered his children's distress at different times, failing an exam or losing a race, a girlfriend. Knowing that they couldn't believe him but still trying to tell them that it would pass, that they would be amazed, looking back, to think it had mattered at all. He thought of himself, thought of things that had seemed so important, so full of meaning when he was twenty, or forty, and he thought maybe it was like one of Jenny's books after all. Red herrings and misdirection, all the characters and observations that seemed so central, so significant while the story was unfolding. But then at the end you realized that the crucial thing was really something else. Something buried in a conversation, a description—you realized that all along it had been a different answer, another person glimpsed but passed over, who was the key to everything. Whatever *everything* was. And if you went back, as Jenny sometimes did, they were there, the clues you'd missed while you were reading, caught up in the need to move forward. All quietly there.

Sometimes, sitting up in bed beside him, Jenny would close her book with a bang and say, *For Heaven's sake, I knew that on page twenty-three.* Or complain about what annoyed her even more, a twist at the end that hadn't been prepared for, that made no sense, given what had gone before. The pleasure seemed to depend on a delicate balance, on letting yourself be fooled, so long as in the end you could see how it had been done. He wasn't as devoted a mystery reader as Jenny had been but he usually finished the ones his neighbor brought from the library. Sometimes there were ancient crumbs trapped between the pages, a sepia stain that might have been from a cup of coffee Jenny had been drinking, years before. Once a hard crust of something that looked like flour and water paste and made him think of the two of them in the kitchen, long past midnight, working on a papier-mâché mountain range someone had to take to school. Their fingers thick with the newspaper mess, and Jenny's forehead crusted where she kept pushing back her hair. *Do you think they'll even remember any of this?* she said.

His first thought was of course they would, remembering the tears of frustration, the vast relief on the face of the child who had gone sleepily up the stairs. But then he thought of rocking a crying baby to sleep, of plates of brownies and sequins sewn on costumes, stories and walks and the endless unfunny jokes and riddles. *Think what you remember,* Jenny said. *What do you really remember, of when you were five, or eight, or ten. Would it be what your parents thought you would remember? What they wanted you to?* And in the paper-strewn kitchen in the middle of the night they talked about how strange it was, that the person you were was perhaps formed most by all that you had forgotten.

· · ·

He had promised his children that when the stairs became too much he would sell the big house they grew up in, would move into someplace more manageable, or maybe even into Ellie's spare room; now that he didn't get around much it didn't really matter what city he lived in. He had promised them and he might actually do it, although he found it hard to imagine. Maybe instead what he thought of as Jenny's last gift, the nearly full bottle of pills rolled up in a pair of socks in his top dresser drawer. Maybe he would go to sleep one night deciding that he'd had enough. Fold his hands, close his eyes, and slide into a dream so deep that no sounds, no swaying shapes, would disturb it. He would leave a note on the outside door for Brenda, telling her who to call. Leave a letter for his children telling them not to mind too much. Telling them that he was glad that he had lived; he was glad for his life.

BOOK

THERE ARE SMUDGES on one of the pages that caused a few tears, but mostly she's happy with it and she knows how pleased they will be, her father and her mother and her sister, turning the pages on Christmas day. The idea had just appeared in her mind, and once it did, it began to tumble and grow and she could hardly keep up, working on one picture with others already nudging at her, needing to be done. Joshua Whippet, the daredevil, swinging from the rough branch of a tree. David Whippet looking out through a window during his long confinement, plump Mother Whippet with her hands pressed to her mouth. She hoped that one would make Lil laugh.

The last page gave her the most trouble, the page of her own family; she wanted them just the way they had been at the photographer's house at the end of the bridge, in the magic room with the painted mountains, the rugs and the ferns in pots, dishes of stones and colored glass. The photographer had such wild hair, a scar or a dimple in one cheek, and the woman who helped him wore a dress the color of her green eyes and said all kinds of crazy things to make them smile while she moved their hands, their heads. Stepping backward out of the light she knocked a pedestal table; it fell with a bang that made them all jump and she called herself a great ninny, said they could call her that too if they liked, and that made even her father smile. They were so happy walking home that day, just happy, with nothing underneath. The photograph would have always reminded them but her father said it hadn't turned out well, said he'd refused to pay for it, and there was something about the look of her mother's mouth as she moved things around in the parlor, filled in the perfect space they'd made for it. There were things Rachel knew nothing about, things she tucked away. Like the day her father brought home a box of paints, sheets of fine paper that were rich beneath her fingertips. Her mother untied her apron and went to her room.

Miss Alice helped with the last picture, although she didn't know it. That way she had of saying something that made you see things in a different way. It was something she said to Nina, who was trying to cut a shape out of folded paper; Miss Alice said something to Nina, and Rachel suddenly understood that the idea of the last picture was beyond what she could do, what she could do at this moment. That was all, and it didn't mean that she had failed, it didn't mean that she would never do it; it just meant that she had to change her idea, move her family out of the glowing studio that was so hard to capture, rearrange them so that the hands, which were giving her so much trouble, didn't really show. She saw how much easier it would be, for now, if she let herself do the things she could do well, and when the picture was finished she made the rest of the book, slicing pieces from a cigar box with Lil's hidden knife for the covers, pounding holes with a nail in the yard behind the shed. She asked her mother for pieces from the rag bag and cut with the heavy scissors, close to the lamp in the center of the kitchen table. The glue pot was almost empty and she had to scrape around with the brush, the tang of it making her wrinkle her nose. *It's something for school,* she said when her mother asked, and that was a lie but she thought not a terrible one, a lie for a good reason.

It was something like a lie that she told Eaton too; there were places she could have hidden the Whippet book, or she could have given it to Miss Alice until Christmas. But for some reason she wanted someone else to see it, someone who wasn't her family or her teacher, someone who wouldn't like it for those reasons. There was something about Eaton, the dreamy look in his eye and the way he didn't tease or pinch, the way he sometimes said things, asked questions that were exactly in her own mind. In Sunday school, Miss Sarah said that even the kindest face could hide an evil heart, and maybe that was true. But if it was, then you couldn't believe anything or anyone, and that meant Miss Sarah too, and that just made it all too complicated. So she gave the book to Eaton and she trusted that he would keep it safe, and in some way it was a gift for him too, and she thought that he would know that. The next morning there was something uneasy in the house but Lil plaited her hair for her, the way she always did, and the moment she stepped out the door the blue day claimed her. Her hair pulled at her scalp a little but it would loosen, and she could picture the bit of red ribbon Lil had tied.

There was a tingle in the air and a wonderful woody smell, and the wheels of a buggy spun as it creaked by, the *clop* of a horse's hooves. Lines from a poem Miss Alice liked were running through her head. *My heart leaps up,* she said to herself. *My heart leaps up.*

EATON—1889

HE WAS SUDDENLY awake and there was nothing else
to explain it. No shreds of a nightmare, no barking dogs,
no sound at all from the house around him. He felt beneath the
pillow for his father's watch, checked the time in the thin slip
of light that lay across his blanket. It was Drifter Dan's method,
the one that had helped him escape from the Indian camp in
The Black Rider, that he had used again when he rescued Clara
Brady from the outlaws. Repeat twenty times before sleep: *I will
wake up at*—

Drifter Dan often slept in his clothes and Eaton thought he
should have done that too, time wasted trying to figure out what
had happened to his buttons, until he understood that the shirt
was inside out. He crept past his parents' rooms, his boots hanging from their knotted laces, and stepped down the edges of the
back stairs. He was a boy who loved to sleep and he couldn't remember ever being the only one awake in the house. First light

just beginning to brush the windows, the dark kitchen with its looming shapes, the pools of deeper darkness that became chairs, the woodstove in the corner, only as he stared at them. It was something he'd never noticed, the way darkness was textured, shaded. Part of the way things seemed to be now, nothing simple, not even the difference between the dark and the light. There was a place he sometimes sat when he was smaller, just around the bend in the back stairs, a place where he could hear things. Hear Lucy singing while she worked, and the things she said after his mother rustled out of the room. The things she talked about when Abby used to come and drink mugs of tea at the kitchen table, in the quiet part of an afternoon. Once she told Abby about going to see the Medium in her rented room above Hatch's grocery. How at first everything was hazy but it slowly became clearer and clearer, until at last she saw her little girl's face. It had worried him then, knowing that Lucy had been to the place Reverend Toller preached so fiercely against. But that was before, when everything was easy. When he didn't know what it was like, to need to see the dead again.

· · ·

One lie was all the Devil needed; that was what Miss Sarah said. What Rachel's father said once when he came to the Sunday school to hear their verses, when he touched Eaton's shoulder with his murderous hand. One lie would open the door a crack, and that was enough for the Devil to come slithering in. He knew that, but he also knew that if he was going to do this thing he had to be long gone before Lucy came through the back door, raked up the stove, before his father straightened his collar and sat down with his knife and fork held lightly in his hands. When he'd gone into the sitting room the night before his voice sounded just the way he'd practiced, saying, *I might go early to-morrow; Miss Alice wants help with something before school.* His parents looked up from their separate pools of light, his mother's hands flowing with jewel green thread, his father with a small book open on his lap. *Good night, Eaton,* was all they said when he bent to kiss their cheeks, and he braced himself for a voice calling him back as he climbed the stairs, but there was only the sound of his light footsteps.

They would find out, of course they would, but he had pushed that thought away, pushed it away now as he felt around in the dark pantry until he found Lucy's ginger cake, wrapped in a clean cloth, only three slices gone. She would be angry, but not for very long, and he saw how true it was that one lie, one thing, led to more and more. The evening of that other day his father sat on the edge of his bed and told him there was nothing wrong with crying but that wasn't the reason; it was just too big a thing for crying. His father said that it wasn't really something that could be understood, that Rachel's father had made a mistake, and then another and another, and the trouble piled up until he must have thought it was the only way out of it. He said that no one could have known and Eaton thought that made it even worse, the idea that anything at all could happen at any time, that there was no one there to stop it.

It makes no sense, he said, and what he meant was that it had been a morning like so many others, around the big table in the schoolroom. Nina was beside Miss Alice, her face scrunched up like it always was when she read aloud, and Rachel was in her place next to him, doing her sums so quickly while he struggled with a problem about bushels of apples. Lucius flicked a plug of paper from across the table and Rachel looked up and stuck her tongue out at him and just then there was knocking at the outside door, not thunderous, not desperate, just knocking. Miss Alice came back and said that Rachel's father needed her for a moment and she put down her pencil, left her book lying open on the table. He saw that out of the corner of his eye as he stroked out a number and started again and he didn't even bother to raise his head as she disappeared through the doorway, walked out into the blue day that swallowed her up. It made no sense that they had all just let her go, that Lucius and Bella had walked right by the house on their way home at lunchtime and there had been nothing for them to notice. It made no sense that no one, not even Miss Alice, had given Rachel more than a passing thought when her chair was empty all afternoon, her book still open on the table. When she was lying dead on her bedroom floor. His father left the lamp burning low that night, left the door ajar, but it made no difference; he still woke screaming.

· · ·

There was a light in the Barnes' kitchen, a shape moving near the window, and he thought it might be Miss Alice, conjured up by his lie. He opened the side door carefully, bending down like Drifter Dan did when he crawled through the flap of the tepee to make his escape. Drifter Dan had been raised by Indians, but a different tribe from the one that tortured him in *The Black Rider*, and again in *Deadman's Gulch;* once he recognized his blood brother, Tuctoya, just as he was about to squeeze the trigger of his Winchester. That was when he was a scout for the army, years after he'd been rescued and brought back to civilization. Back to a place he didn't remember, where he had to keep his hands clean and sit at a desk in a schoolhouse. Drifter Dan always knew that wherever he was, he only half belonged.

Eaton crouched as low as he could and eased the door closed behind him, counting to twenty before he let it move each fraction. The green smell of wet grass was all around him, slippery on his hands as he made his way around the back of the house, and water from the bushes on the other side dampened his cheek, his shoulder. Then he was standing up and the street was wide open in front of him. He made himself walk slowly, clutching the cloth-wrapped cake against his stomach, made himself move like someone who had every right to be there. The dark was unraveling a little more, first birds stirring, a call and then another, but it was still too early for anyone to be about. No one sweeping a front step, no silent men on their way to the factory, no wagons rattling toward the station. It felt like walking through a ghost town, like being the only thing left alive in a place people had built and then left behind.

· · ·

They were meeting behind the Murder House and when he peeked around the corner Shiner was already there, sitting on the back steps, looking like he wasn't bothered. Like they were any back steps leading to any back door. One night during the trial the sound of breaking glass splintered the night and now all the windows were boarded up, another thing that made it strange, and not like a place where a family had ever lived. He thought about how dark it would be behind those boards, real darkness, and he thought about all the things sealed up inside. Beds and chairs and dishes on a table, a book, a newspaper, a jacket hanging on a hook. Like the empty street, rutted by vanished wagons, lined with solid houses, it was a place with only the life sucked out.

There'd be bloodstains too, inside in the dark, and he knew just where, knew where their bodies had fallen. His mother didn't agree but his father gave him the newspaper to read, said there would be all kinds of wild stories and it would be better if he knew the facts. He read that Rachel made a sound when Constable Street turned her over, that she seemed to move, though she was quite cold, and Eaton ran down the hall, stood in the doorway of his father's office and said, *She was alive; it says here she was alive.* His father explained in a quiet voice about bodies and gases, how someone who didn't know could be mistaken. He said of course he would have saved her if he could, would have saved them all.

· · ·

Shiner said he'd been there all night and maybe he had; his hair was pearled with dew but the step showed bone dry when he shifted over to make room. They ate the ginger cake, saving a bit for Will although neither of them thought he would really come. Then they were thirsty, and the pump screamed when Eaton moved the handle. They were ready to run but no one shouted, no one came, so they drank a little but the water was rusty, bloody tasting. Shiner spat it out too, and he wasn't afraid of anything. The first time they met him he was crying but that was because he was hurt, his nose a bloody mess and a small white tooth lying in the dust. Eaton and Will might have passed by, except for the story of the Good Samaritan. Shiner jumped up with his fists clenched when they stopped, but he didn't hit out at them. He said he'd had money from carrying bags at the station, that he'd get even worse if he went home with empty pockets, but they had nothing to give him. Instead they told him about the place where they'd found frogs, hundreds of frogs, and he said he didn't mind if they showed him. It was just Eaton's bad luck that when he came home, late for dinner again, his mother was watching for him, came into the kitchen and saw the state of his boots, his muddy clothes. She made Lucy drag out the tub and fill it and she scrubbed him herself, stinging his skin, until she got tired. Later, Lucy came up the back stairs with a wedge of bread and butter, smoothed his hair and didn't say a word about the extra work he'd caused her.

. . .

He hadn't dared to bring the watch but Shiner said they didn't need it, said they'd hear a wagon or two near the time the first train was due, and that would be their signal. Then Eaton remembered that Prince would be shifting his feet in his stall, hungry and waiting, but it was too late to go back, too close to the time when stoves would be heating, people stepping into the day. Another thing he'd be punished for, but he didn't mind that part so much. It was the thought of Prince's big dark eyes, the way his ears would be twitching at every sound, trusting in someone who had forgotten all about him.

The ginger cake turned heavy in his stomach and the wooden step was hard; he looked out at the murky yard and thought about the bloodstained house behind his back. The last time he was in this yard it was another season, one of those days that seemed to last forever. At the Band of Hope meeting after church he sat in his usual place, beside know-it-all Robert Bride with his poker-straight back, behind Rachel. There was a faint smell of flowers that he thought came from her, and it reminded him of something. Miss Sarah paced in front of them, telling one of her stories about a happy family, a family that could be their own, and how it had crumbled, the children hungry, begging on the streets, because of King Alcohol. When she turned toward the window sunlight flashed from her spectacles, as if she was signaling to someone. He watched her pace, flash, turn, pace flash turn, until his eyelids were terribly heavy and he made himself break the spell, remembering what had happened that time Little Jonah fell asleep and slid right off his chair.

He tried to concentrate on Miss Sarah's voice but the words couldn't hold him, the story so familiar, so like all her stories. He tried counting instead, to one hundred by twos, by fives and back again, keeping his eyes on Rachel's head in front of him. And then he thought of touching her hair. He didn't do it, but for some reason he thought of it, saw his hand with its bitten-down nails tracing the weave of her long, dark plait that seemed to shine in the same sunlight that erased Miss Sarah's eyes. Just for a moment he thought that, and then chairs scraped as everyone stood up, Miss Sarah swooping her left hand back and forth through the air while they sang "Joyful Be Our Numbers" loud enough to wake every drunkard in town.

Later that afternoon, while Lucy clattered in the kitchen, while his mother slept, her upper lip sprinkled with sugar, he found himself approaching Rachel's house. He didn't know why, just as he didn't know why he'd taken a scout's route to get there. Around two blocks, down the back lane, through the gap in the fence next door and then bent down, almost on hands and knees, into the tangle of the raspberry patch that marked the edge of the Heaths' yard. The dry canes rattled, but he moved so slowly that anyone would have thought it was the wind.

Rachel's sister was in the yard, crouched down by the side of the chicken coop, out of sight of the house. At first he thought she was looking for something she'd dropped, or that maybe she was planting seeds, like Miss Alice in the school garden. The way her fingers were scrabbling in the dirt. He crept closer, placing each foot carefully, holding his breath until he was as near as he dared to be. Until he could see her fingers in the earth, see the way she raised them to her mouth, a glimpse of her white teeth. The way her lips closed, her jaw moved once or twice, the way she swallowed. The smudges on her chin.

He must have made a sound, some sound, for she was suddenly very still. She raised her eyes and they looked at each other through a mesh of dead canes, maybe eight feet apart, maybe only six. And he couldn't move and she didn't move and it seemed they would be frozen that way forever, not even breathing, locked to each other forever. Until a bird cawed, a door opened, a voice called her name. And he scrambled to his feet and began to run, things snatching at him, running faster, tearing his Sunday shirt on the splintered fence, running as if something was right behind him.

· · ·

He thought about telling Shiner what he'd seen that day, but something in him was uneasy about saying it out loud. It was one of those things, and there seemed to be more and more of them, that floated around in his head, things he didn't have a place to put. Every day Rachel went to meet her father coming home and they walked together, her father looking down at her, Rachel looking up. They walked together like that every day, like two people who loved each other more than anything. Eaton had that picture in his head, and he couldn't get it to fit with what had happened. Shiner's father, so free with his fists and boots, that would have made some sense, but Shiner was still alive, sitting beside him on the hard wooden step while the daylight opened up the yard, the loose-boarded shed, the leftover stalks of last year's garden.

Shiner said his father had told him about a hanging he'd seen when he was a boy, sitting on his own father's shoulders. He said that in those days a beam jutted from the second floor of the courthouse, that a man just stepped out into the air, spun and danced at the end of a rope while everyone cheered. He'd seen another hanging when he was older, before they built the wall around the jail. Told Shiner how the man was wailing like a woman, had to be dragged up the thirteen steps to the scaffold. But Rachel's father wouldn't die like that either. There was a new method, described in the newspaper, involving pulleys and a heavy weight. A scientific method, the newspaper said, and not so cruel. The day before Eaton had walked by the jail after school, heard hammer blows ringing out and thought about Rachel's father in his dungeon, hearing the same thing. His father had told his mother that Mr. Heath didn't say a word, those times he went to check him over. Just sat on his cot, looking down at his clasped hands. Eaton thought that might have been in one of his nightmares, the clasped hands with their odd long fingernails. He thought about what it would be like, hearing a normal sound like nails knocking into wood and knowing it was the sound of your death. Wishing, probably wishing that you'd used that last bullet, that you hadn't been taken alive.

It was one of Shiner's brothers who had found him, his brother Mick, up to something in the heart of the wood, in a spot the sun rarely reached. He'd heard the news in town and thought there might be a reward; otherwise he would have just kept going. A man with a gun in the shadows no business of his. But he'd heard the news and so he went for the constable, running when he thought he was far enough away, tripping twice, his hands covered with leaf slime. He had to convince Street, convince the others who promised him a hiding and a night in the cells if he was up to his usual tricks. A thick fist bunched in the neck of his shirt as he led them back, certain that Heath would have fled, that he would be for it.

But Heath hadn't fled, was sitting in exactly the same spot, leaning against the rough bark of the oak tree. His hands dangling, one holding the gun, his eyes open but not seeming to look at anything. The big men hunkered down, whispered a plan, and Mick slipped away back to town, quite forgetting why he'd gone there in the first place. He told Luft from the newspaper that he'd exchanged words with Heath, but that they made no sense and he couldn't remember what they were. A number of people told Luft that they'd seen Heath that day, or in the days before, that his eyes were dark and mad, flecks of foam on his lips. But Mick told Shiner that he'd looked just like always, only maybe a little sadder.

．　．　．

They couldn't wait any longer for Will, so Shiner ate the last of the cake and then tied the wrapping around his face like an outlaw. *Stick 'em up,* he said, pointing his finger at Eaton, the white cloth sucking into his mouth and then releasing. *Don't shoot,* Eaton said, in a high, squeaky voice. *I'll give you all the gold.* Shiner knew everything about cowboys, and he had a plan to light out for the Wild West as soon as his mother was better. They played train robbery and posse all over town, in the empty bandshell, down by the river, or often in Quint's woods. Once they tied Will to a stripling tree, tied him tight with a piece of rope Shiner had around his waist. He was a captive, about to be tortured, and they would ride to save him in the nick of time. Will got them to scatter bits of twigs and dried grass around in a circle; all his favorite games had fire in them. Joan of Arc at the stake, Shadrach-Meshach-Abednego in the blazing furnace. He called out *Help help, save me,* as they ran from the clearing, and without even talking about it they kept on running until they were tired and flopped down in the long grass in Badgers' Field, the sun hot on their upturned faces. *Serves him right,* Shiner said, after a while. Shiner went to school as often as he had to and he said that the last caning he got was for drawing a rude picture on the teacher's blotter. He said he knew who had really done it but Will hadn't said a word, just sat watching like all the rest. *Serves him right,* Shiner said again. *Hear that?* And Eaton thought he heard a faint voice still calling, calling their names.

When they went back later, much later, Will was gone, the rope still looped in loose coils around the tree. That made it a different kind of thing but Will never mentioned it, and neither did they. Eaton flinched from the thought whenever it came to him, burned with shame when he remembered the extra tug he had given, tightening the knot, the glee he had felt, running away.

• • •

They knew how to move through the town without being seen. Through back lanes, bent low beneath windows, along the narrow alleyways between stores. Drifter Dan knew an Indian trick, wrapped himself in dusty skins to creep up on something and they tried that once, tugging down a blanket that was airing on a line, but Mrs. Bell came shouting through her back door and they had to run for their lives.

There was a little round man who got off the train every month or so with cases of ribbons and hair combs that he sold to

Becks', to other places in town. His cases weren't heavy, but if Shiner carried them right up to his room he gave him a few of the thin-paper novels, stories about Drifter Dan and Buffalo Bill, about detectives like Old King Carter, about the Dane brothers, who were masters of disguise. Shiner could read but he was slow so he gave them to Eaton, sometimes to Will, said they could just tell him what happened. Eaton's mother threw *Whiskey Sam* into the fire, and then he had to keep the books under the straw in a corner of Prince's stall; a horsey, Wild West smell rose when he turned the pages.

Shiner called the round man Old Filthy, and sometimes when he put the latest novels in Eaton's hands he said, *You still love them, don't you?* In the stories the evildoers had glittering eyes and sallow faces, sometimes a mustache thin as a pen stroke. It was easy to tell them apart from the innocent townsfolk, and they always came to a bad end, even if it took several episodes.

The three of them didn't have reversible clothes and wigs but they taught themselves how to follow people just like the Dane brothers did, like Jim Wise, Boy Detective. It wasn't easy; the first time a man with big hands spun around and grabbed Shiner, gave him a shake and said he'd tan his hide. When they were together it was always Shiner who drew the trouble. It wasn't fair at all, but no one seemed able to know that it was usually Will who was behind the worst things. Dropping a lit match in the long grass at the edge of the fairgrounds, tipping over a bin of flour in Hatch's grocery. Once throwing a rock that startled a horse and ended up with two wagons overturned on the road, splintered wood and a man with blood dripping down his face. Before his mother died Will wouldn't even spit but now he was up to all kinds of things, wild and sneaky things. More and more careless, and Eaton was sure that one of these times people who would never have thought it would have to see, and then he would be sorry. He would have to be sorry.

. . .

Even from the back lane they could hear sounds of the town awake, and when they came carefully out of the alley beside McAdam's hardware store it was like a photograph come to life, horses, buggies, a dog or two, and people walking quickly. Right across from them was Marl's pharmacy, the swirly gold lettering on the deep blue sign, and Eaton looked, like he always did, for the ghostly *B* that still showed through from when it used to be Barnes'. His father had showed him that once when he was smaller, and it must have been his father who told him that the store belonged to Miss Alice's father, before he died. That some people thought, his father thought, that Mr. Marl could have waited a little longer before painting over his name. That had something to do with why Eaton went to the Barnes' school, and not to the new stone building on the hill. Mrs. Barnes was fluttery and strange but Miss Alice had a way of talking, a way of explaining that led you to the answer without even thinking that it was hard to find. She had a way of saying your name that made you feel you were important to her, and when he first went to school he used to wonder what it would be like if she was his mother. He couldn't imagine her cross, couldn't imagine her scraping skin with a hard brush, her face all red and dripping from the rising steam. He knew, though, that it wasn't a right thought to have, so he changed it to an older sister. Someone connected to him who would give him hugs and tease him, who would muss his hair but always look out for him, always take his part. And he thought maybe his older sister would make his mother happier too. Someone who wouldn't tangle the wool when she held it to wind, someone who wouldn't mind carrying her basket from store to store on a sunny Saturday. Someone she could talk to, instead of being quiet behind the closed door of her room.

Miss Sarah was Miss Alice's older sister, but except for their faces they were nothing alike. Miss Sarah reminded him of the angles they had to draw with a ruler and sharp pencil, all straight, hard lines. Men laughed at her, standing outside Malley's with a fistful of pamphlets, but she was too fierce to feel sorry for. Sometimes at the Band of Hope she made her voice go soft and kind but that was just a trick, just the way she made her stories work. Starting off with a happy family around a dinner table, beside the fire, a world that made you think nothing bad could ever happen.

Rachel's sister was peculiar; he'd heard that even before he saw her swallowing down dirt in the bare yard. But the two of them often sat together on their front porch and he'd heard them talking, heard Rachel talking anyway, nothing in her voice to say she was doing it in a special way, in a way you might talk to a dog or a baby that couldn't understand. Mostly that was where Rachel was after school, sitting on the porch with her sister Lil, or somewhere inside the house. She wasn't one of those girls who plaited flowers on the riverbank, sometimes hiking their skirts almost to their knees and shrieking in the cold, green water. The ones he and Will, Shiner too, liked to ambush, bursting out of the trees with fierce war cries, sending them scattering. Once they came whooping and the girls didn't scream, did nothing at all but carry on talking, placing wreaths on each other's heads. Until Shiner scooped up a handful of spring mud, threw it with a splat that landed on a white sleeve. Mud flying everywhere, the girls throwing it back, until a stone hit Bella in the nose and made her cry. Running back to the trees they heard her shouting, *You filthy* **boys**, *you filthy disgusting* **boys***!*

Rachel wasn't one of those girls but she could have been; everyone liked her, and she was never ignored outside the church on a Sunday morning. But except for the schoolroom Eaton only saw her sitting with her sister Lil, or walking with her mother or her father. Once in a while by herself on the walk in front of their house, bouncing a ball and clapping twice, clapping three times before she caught it. Not long after they came to town she did once call to him from her front porch and they played jack-straws, their heads almost touching as they hunched together, sliding the sticks from the jumbled pile. Rachel was good at it; she looked and looked before she did anything, seemed to know which sticks didn't matter and which were the important ones, holding everything in place. *Not that one,* she said, but he eased it out anyway and the whole thing came tumbling down. On her next turn she looked and looked, and then suddenly she said, *There's my papa!* Jumped to her feet, the toe of her boot scattering the pile, snapping one thin stick into pieces, and ran down the step, ran to where a dark-dressed shape was just rounding a far corner, and the shape bent forward, maybe touched her forehead with his own, before they came slowly down the street together.

· · ·

Eaton and Shiner stepped boldly now, enough people around to cover them, and made their way along the sidewalk. Right at McAdam's, right again at the bank on the next corner, past the market square and toward the high-walled jail. It reminded Eaton of going to the fair, or the time Lucy took him to the revival tent. Something in the way people greeted each other, in the sound of their voices, the way their eyes flicked from face to face. A kind of hum, a sense of everything stretched so tightly it might even snap. Like Drifter Dan in *The Wolf on the War-Path,* he emptied his mind so that he could take in everything, all his senses honed. The hum was in Shiner's voice too when he said, *Come on,* twisting his way through the crowd in the street, turning to see that Eaton was following. He was suddenly glad that Will had funked it, although he was someone he saw almost every day of his life, someone whose house he knew as well as his own. He had once sobbed in Will's kitchen; he couldn't remember why, only that Mrs. Toller was still alive, that she had put her arms around him, rocked him back and forth, made a joke while they both dried their eyes.

Will's father would have thundered if he knew about the hours spent with Shiner, and that was maybe part of why he'd stayed away. Everyone knew them, knew all three, and someone would be bound to say. It was true that Shiner was good at filching candy, at sliding sweet buns up his sleeve. True that he was often in fights, but only with a reason. There was no reason in the things Will sometimes did, the things that just seemed to burst out of him. He smiled sweetly when the town ladies asked how he did, poor motherless boy, and sometimes he was like he used to be, but even then there was a possibility of wildness just held in, of something that could swirl loose at any moment. That's how it seemed to Eaton. Like a horse that would stand still and nuzzle your hand, then suddenly kick out a mean, sharp hoof.

. . .

From away by the river the church bell rang seven, and he felt each clang to the toes of his dusty boots. A man with a crumpled black hat was arguing in a doorway with two other men, who were shouting with their hands on their hips. One walked away but the other took something from his pocket and the crumpled man moved aside, pointing up the stairway behind him. Looking up, Eaton saw that the low ridge on the rooftop was lined with faces. When he looked back Shiner was gone but he didn't panic, used his scout sense to scan for the gray shirt and finally found him right by the wall of the jail, talking to his brother. Not Mick but the oldest one, Bash, who had been in jail for cutting a woman with a knife. Shiner was asking for money to get onto the roof and his brother threw a silver coin in the air but caught it just out of his reach, laughed a hard laugh as his hand closed around it. Shiner spat on the ground, but not until Bash was almost across the street. *I know a better place anyway,* he said, and they followed the wall to the corner, chose the tree with the lowest branches, Shiner's hard, bare foot pushing off from Eaton's clasped hands as he boosted him up.

· · ·

When he was younger, he sometimes went out with his father. Not on his calls in town but on longer rides, along dusty roads, through twisting tracks with overhanging trees. Sometimes they sang songs and sometimes Eaton sat on his father's lap and held the reins, but he couldn't really drive because Prince was younger then too, and unpredictable. Once his father told him about a friend he'd had, and how they competed for everything, even the same girl. *But you won,* Eaton said, and his father smiled. Then he said that one of these times they'd bring fishing poles, see if they could catch a big fish and Lucy would cook it for their supper.

Sometimes Eaton's father would bring him inside and the

farm women would make a fuss over the Doctor's boy, sit him at a table with a plate of bread and jam. Sometimes he had to wait outside in the buggy, and the waiting could go on and on. Once they drove up a long lane, and when they came near the square stone house there was a woman standing by the wall, her apron pulled up over her face. She brought her hands down, came to meet them when she heard their turning wheels; her face had more freckles than Eaton had ever seen, and he wondered if that was why she was hiding. That was one of the times his father told him to wait in the buggy and he did, but it was a very long time. He was so thirsty waiting, and he thought that it would be all right if he looked for a pump or a well behind the quiet house. He didn't find a pump, but he did find a freckle-faced boy about his own size, and they climbed an apple tree, pelted each other with the hard, green fruit, and chased around the barn a few times. The boy said there were kittens inside and they opened a creaking door, climbed a rough wooden ladder up to the hay, and lay on their stomachs looking at the nest the striped cat had circled out for herself, the wet, blind things squeaking around her. *Next time you come, you can take one home,* the boy said, his face so close that Eaton could feel the breath of his words.

His father's calling was angry and his foot slipped going down the ladder; he almost fell, and that made him run faster, back to the waiting buggy. There was a small sack at his father's feet and when Eaton opened it he saw wizened potatoes, smelled something rotten. *They're no good,* he said, and his father told him it didn't matter, told him that you had to take what people were able to give you, even if it wasn't what you really wanted.

The next time his father led Prince out of the stable Eaton asked if they could go to the boy's house to get a kitten, but his father said no. And when he kept pestering his father slapped the side of the buggy, said he'd been wrong to take Eaton there at all. He said they'd talk about it later but days went by, the kittens all the time growing into cats, and they never did.

• • •

Shiner climbed a little higher in the tree and hung from his bent knees, his upside-down face moving between the leaves. It made Eaton think of the magic lantern Will's father had and the way the pictures flickered, Mother Goose on her gander, Samson with the temple crashing down. When he had told Miss Alice about it once, she said that she would show them something even more amazing. After lunch, she led them into the back kitchen, dark because she'd draped a black cloth tight over the only window. She told them to stand on that side, facing the opposite, whitewashed wall, to stand still, let their eyes get used to the murky light, and look straight at the wall. What Eaton saw first was hazy, something shifting, that was no color he could put a name to. *Keep looking,* Miss Alice said, out of the gloom, and just as someone whispered, *I see it,* he saw it too. Something square and beside it a shape in the softest green, still shimmering but coming clearer as he looked. *What is it?* Rachel said, and then one of the young ones said, *A clue, can we have a clue please, Miss? One clue,* Miss Alice said. *It's upside down.*

One clue was enough, and Eaton blinked and knew it. *A tree,* he said, *it's a tree upside down,* and he knew it so surely that he couldn't believe that just a moment before he hadn't. *And a building with windows,* someone said, maybe Rachel again, *an upside-down building. Do you all see it?* Miss Alice said, and they all said they did, though Nina didn't sound sure. Then Miss Alice climbed on a chair and pulled down the black cloth and they all saw through the window, saw the green slope down to the river, the bulk of the stone factory on the other side, the dense plume of the maple tree just at the corner of it, all bathed in the light of the high sun.

Miss Alice said it was Science, said they all knew that sunlight was made up of colors, didn't they? They did, most of them did, and she told them that the light of day bounced around all in a jumble, colors flying here and there and all mixed up. Then she said that she'd made the whole room into something like a magic lantern, maybe more like a camera; someone had shown her the same thing once. She showed them a hole she had made in the black cloth, explained that when the sunlight could only come in that one hole, it meant that only a bit of each color could get through. That was why they saw the tree, the stone wall of the factory, even though those things were behind them, and turned the other way. She couldn't remember why they were upside down but she said that what they had seen was real, not magic, although it was very like magic. That the trembling tree, the building, were always there, that they just needed a way to be seen. They did it over and over, the boys taking turns on the chair, fixing the heavy dark cloth and taking it down again, seeing the same picture, a little more of it each time.

He remembered that, looking at Shiner's leaf-dappled face, remembered that he had thought about it for hours, maybe for days. If they were there all the time, the factory and the tree, then so was the river, so were the houses, every person walking about. And that meant, that had to mean, that he was walking all the time through a hazy, upside-down world, that the empty air was filled with quivering shapes, just waiting to be revealed, that every solid thing in the world had a ghostly opposite. He thought about it for days and then set it aside, not able to understand how it could really be.

. . .

There were more people than on the busiest market day in the street around the closed front gate, and faces peered over the rooftops across the way. Three young men had climbed the tree after them, and wouldn't let anyone else up. They were talking loudly about a dance they'd been to, and someone named Chas who was sweet on a girl named Louisa, how he never went anywhere now unless she gave permission. An old man walking beneath heard their shouting laughter, looked up and shook his cane, called them ghouls and said why didn't they get jobs instead of carousing all hours, instead of finding entertainment in watching some poor wretch lose his life. The young men just laughed more, and one of them tried to tear off twigs to pelt the angry man. But the twigs were green and bent instead of breaking, a handful of stripped-off leaves floating down to land in the space he'd already left.

I'm a ghoul too, Shiner said, hunching his shoulders and rubbing his hands together, twisting his face. Eaton copied him, but he didn't think that was the whole reason he had made the plan. The rest of it was something he didn't seem to have a choice about, something he was caught up in. Something that must have started with the murders, because he found it hard to remember a time before.

It seemed to be all about waiting, this day, and in the tree he thought again that it was a good thing Will hadn't come, thought about what it would have been like with that high voice chattering in his ear. Shiner said that Will just talked for the sake of hearing his own voice, and not much of what he said meant anything at all. He had said that the day they were supposed to hunt buffalo with Will's real bow and arrows, Shiner waiting out of sight while Eaton knocked on the heavy front door. Will said he couldn't come and closed the door quickly, before Eaton had a chance to ask if they could take the bow anyway. Before the door slammed he heard Reverend Toller's voice, talking in a church way. Sometimes the whole family had to spend the day on their knees.

The bows they'd made themselves didn't work very well, the arrows plunking to the ground far short of the cows grazing in Arnold's pasture. They left them lying there and went into the woods to look for more feathers, and Shiner said it was nice, just the two of them. Shiner didn't talk much usually, and he didn't like to explain the ideas he had. Usually he'd just charge off into something and Eaton and Will would follow, figuring it out as the game went along. He could run like the wind and he could fight if he had to, and he had the loudest yell of all of them, sending pigeons flapping through the dusty sunlight in Ridley's falling-down barn. But sometimes he went completely still, seemed to disappear behind his own eyes. The way he did that would help him when he went to the Wild West, would make him a good scout, a good hunter. But Eaton didn't like it, it even scared him a little, the way Shiner could remove himself. Something like Eaton's father, when he raised his eyes from a book, turned from a twilight window. The way he had to blink a few times before he was really there, before he realized who was talking to him.

· · ·

Drifter Dan could sit for hours without moving, even when a rattlesnake slithered right across his boot. Eaton wriggled to settle himself, his back against the smooth main trunk, his legs drawn up, feet resting on a solid branch. Shiner had his own branch and was digging at it with his penknife, bending to blow bits of tree dust from the cuts. Eaton stared at his moving hand, the scratching blade, until they started to shimmy a little, until he noticed a far-off buzzing in his ears. He bent his head to touch his knees, the way his father had shown him once when he almost fainted. That was the morning of the funerals, when he sat at the breakfast table and everything looked strangely sharp-edged, the sound of the cutlery echoing, the sound of Lucy's footsteps. He didn't think he'd said anything but maybe his father was looking at him, his cool hand suddenly on the back of Eaton's neck, his calm voice saying, *Put your head down. Put it down.* His new trousers were scratchy against his forehead, his cheek, and as he noticed that he realized he was feeling better, sat up slowly, saying, *I'm all right,* in answer to his father's question. He opened his eyes to a frozen scene, his mother's finger curled in the handle of her teacup, Lucy standing still, two white plates held in her raised hands. But just as quickly as he noticed it the scene changed, moved. His mother raised her cup, drank; his father picked up his napkin from the floor and sat down again in his chair. Lucy stepped forward with her plates, and the glistening yellow eyes of the eggs stared back at him. He didn't think he could bear to touch them with his fork, see them burst and flow. He tore off bits of dry toast and put one in his mouth where it thickened, hard to swallow. It was a thing that made his mother cross, when he picked at his food, but that morning she just said, *You don't have to do this. We could find someone else.*

For a moment the possibility was there, but he knew it was a coward's moment, closed it down. She had said the same thing in his room the night before, laying out his clothes, and she hugged him after she said it, his face crumpled into the slippery stuff of her dress, her smell both sweet and a little tart. Just as he felt himself begin to soften into her, she let him go, with a little push on his shoulder, and he took a deep breath. Sometimes, to his shame, what he most wanted was to curl up in her lap, the way he must have done when he was very small.

From across the table his father said, *It will be fine. You re-member how I explained it?* He nodded his head, the toast paste in his mouth making it impossible to speak. His father had said that they were honoring Rachel by carrying her coffin, Eaton and Lucius and Nina's older brothers. He explained exactly how it would be, where they would sit, what they would have to do, and when. Eaton nodded again when his father asked if he was all right now, egg dripping from the end of his fork.

Excused from the table, he sat on the back step, his arms around his drawn-up knees. Everything was stiff, the unfamiliar trousers, the newly starched shirt, and his skin beneath felt scraped raw, as if the slightest touch might make it bleed. He was tired beyond even knowing it, the last nights filled with tossing dreams. A fiend chasing him down a dark hallway and then appearing suddenly in front of him, turning slowly to re-veal a version of his father's face, pointed teeth dripping blood. At the table he had told his father that he was all right, but he knew that wasn't so, knew that nothing would ever be right again. Rachel had given him her book to hide, the book she was making as a present for Christmas. And now she was dead and he couldn't give it back, and her mother was dead, her sister Lil. There was no one to give it back to, and he didn't know what to do. Only her father left, his eyes glowing in the dark dungeon, and it didn't seem right that he should have it. Just days before, Reverend Toller had read the story of Abraham; he pointed to the stained-glass window and the light falling through that same window made his pointing hand glow red. He had talked about Abraham's anguish, knowing that he would have to slay his only son, but he didn't say anything about what it was like for Isaac, tied to the altar, looking up at the knife in his own father's hand. Isaac lived and that was supposed to make it all right, but what was it like for him, walking back down the mountain at his father's side? What kind of dreams did Isaac have?

Eaton knew that they were in Heaven, Rachel and her mother and her sister, and he knew that was the part he was supposed to think about. How everything was peaceful and they were happy in Heaven, looking down on him, on everyone, with their hair flowing loose, soft wings, with light all around. He knew that at that very moment Rachel was looking down, that she was looking down at him, smiling, with a big hole in her head.

. . .

From where they were they could see the apparatus, the raw new wood that had been sliced from a tree growing tall and straight, maybe somewhere not far away. A tree that, growing, looked just like all the other ones around it, the ones that would make kitchen tables or a little boy's sled, the house that he lived in. The crossbeam was high, and sun flashed now and then on the pulley the rope ran through. One end of the rope canted over to the upright, ran down the side and merged into a tangle of other ropes, some of them holding the weight the newspaper had described, hanging ten feet off the ground. The other end was the noose, dangling down in the middle at a man's height. It looked just like the picture of the noose that had been around Drifter Dan's neck on the cover of *Fiends of the Wild West* and that gave Eaton a start, like something that was just a story had come to life.

Shiner said the Hangman would have come on the midnight train, his hat pulled low so no one could see his face. A shiny black case carrying his own coiled rope, the one that they now saw hanging, completely still. He said that the Hangman traveled from place to place, as he was needed. That no one knew what his real name was, that he was notified by a coded message in the newspaper, the same way King Carter got in touch with the Boy Detective. Between times he lived alone in a tall dark house, and who knew what he did? Counted his piles of gold or cracked small animals' bones, or strung up unlucky strangers for practice.

. . .

Eaton decided it was more like a fair than a revival after all. Loud voices and laughter and the men lower down in their tree trying to make each other fall. But they must have been listening hard all the same; the squeak of the door hinge was not very loud but they all fell silent as a group of men filed out of the jail, crossed the yard and stood near the scaffold. Maybe ten or twelve of them, most in dark coats, most with familiar faces.

There was still a low rumble from the crowd outside the front gate, but then someone gave one shrill whistle and that stopped too. The eight o'clock bell began to toll and while the last stroke still shivered, Reverend Toller appeared in his long white robes, a book open in his hands, and there was a hiss of indrawn breath that seemed to come from everywhere. Rachel's father was behind him, his neck looking strange, no collar on his shirt. His arms were bound behind his back, the same way he held them when he paced in the Sunday school, listening to them recite their verses. The sheriff was a little behind and to the side, one hand out as if to steady, but although Heath walked slowly, he didn't stumble. Behind the sheriff, two jailers in their uniforms, and between them a man with short, carroty hair, wrists hanging out of a too-small jacket. Then Eaton's father and that gave him a start, like seeing the noose. He must have known his father would be there but he hadn't really thought about it and he watched him now, keeping pace with the procession, and remembered him reading in his chair the night before, remembered him saying good night, just like any other time.

It was not a long walk but it seemed to go on and on, each moment filled with things he noticed, spilling into the next, into each other. There was a call from the rooftop across, cut off, and Heath's head jerked up, then bowed down again. Reverend Toller was reading aloud and Eaton realized that he'd been reading since the door squealed open, the murmur of the words now beginning to separate and stand clear. *Man that is born . . . full of misery . . . fleeth as it were a shadow . . .*

Reverend Toller stepped to one side and continued to read, his eyes on the page, although he must have known the words by heart. Heath stopped beneath the dangling noose, and the red-haired man stepped forward, a thick strap in his hand. *That's never the Hangman,* Eaton heard Shiner say, but even as he did the strap was wrapped around Heath's pin-striped legs, drawn tight; he was facing the wall but the man turned him, carefully, to face the jail yard, the silent, black-suited men. *In the midst of life . . .*

The sheriff stepped up and spoke close to Heath's ear, but Heath shook his head once, and he stepped back again. The Hangman placed a black hood over his head—where had that come from? He reached and looped the noose over it, and even from where they were they could see it shake in his hand. *O holy and merciful Savior* . . .

The red-haired man stepped back and stood by the hanging weight, and like in a dream, in a nightmare, something sharp suddenly glinted in his raised hand. *Our father* . . . and Eaton wasn't even breathing, wasn't thinking. *Thy will be done* . . . and the sharp thing flashed again, the weight fell with a heavy thud, a puff of dust. Heath jerked up but only a little way, just as quickly down again, his pointing feet a breath away from the ground.

· · ·

His toes were a ragged breath from the ground and they were moving, and their movement caused him to turn a little, at the end of the rope. His hands were moving too, clenching and opening. At first, Eaton thought it was an escape he was seeing, what a horse might do, having blown out its belly while the cinch was tightened. What King Carter did, craftily turning his hands so the palms faced out while the villains bound them, able to slip free the first time they were distracted. But he thought that only for a moment; the silent world was filled with a terrible groaning sound and it was clear that there was no escape, even though the feet were still moving, the fingers of the bound hands twitching and flicking, frantic.

Someone in the tree said, *Jesus,* in a whisper that rasped like the noises coming from the black hood. The black hood that moved, part of it did, the cloth sucking in and out with the groaning. The red-haired man bolted back toward the jail; the sheriff lifted a hand as if to stop him, but let it fall again. Some of the dark-coated men turned their backs, some still faced straight ahead, and all had their hands clenched tight at their sides.

And it went on and on and on, the jerking and the straining and the black cloth sucking in and out, longer than any buggy wait, longer than any thundering sermon in the stifling summer church, longer than the longest dream-torn night. It went on and on, and then Eaton's father stepped forward and touched the bound man's hands. *He's going to cut him loose,* Shiner breathed, and Eaton flicked his eyes, Shiner's face as pale as cream, maybe his own was too; he said, *No, he's going to check his pulse,* though he didn't know how he knew that. But his father didn't do either of those things, not then. Instead he slipped his hands between Heath's, clasped them tight and they clasped back; Eaton could see it from the tree. Thought he could. And the terrible dancing feet slowed, stopped, the groans lower and longer until they stopped too, and everything was very quiet. Only the tumbling thoughts in Eaton's head, spinning and making their own kind of noise and telling him that he'd been wrong, all wrong about the plan, that nothing was over. He had worked it all out, like Drifter Dan would have, but high in the tree he knew that the success of his plan had only thrown him into another kind of nightmare, that it was the farthest thing from what he really wanted. He tried to take deep breaths, the way he did when he woke in his own bed in the dark, and down in the jail yard his father shifted his hands, one now holding Heath's black-sleeved arm, two fingers of the other pressed inside the rope, the way he'd shown Eaton how to count pulse beats. But there were no beats to count; the sheriff took out his watch, said *Eight fifteen,* and one of the watching men wrote in a notebook. Then they filed back across the yard toward the invisible door, two jailers remaining beside the hanging man, his hooded head drooping forward, the black body stark as a carefully drawn comma.

Eaton's father looked up as he neared the wall, seemed to look straight at him. And Eaton didn't duck, didn't move; he held his father's gaze for what seemed like a long time, thinking that if he could only understand what it was telling him, it would be a thing he would know for the rest of his life.

TREES

THERE ARE TREES in the old world, trees in the new world, some so deep in the heart of things that they've never been seen but still living, changing, touched by wind and rain and the skittering of tiny claws. Others closer to the world of men, and even trapped within it. Some have been started by design, but most are completely random, a seed blown by a breeze or a gale, or passed through the belly of a songbird. Parts can be named—crown, trunk, root—but each one grows in its own way, and some are twisted and stunted by the ones that surround them, while others burst up and through. Even the unseen trees are marked, by disease, by accident, by the paths of gnawing insects, and they grow around their wounds, and are changed by them. Others are marked by climbing children, notches cut and twigs broken off, and the thoughts of small boys are caught in the web of their branches. Some falling with the leaves, some slipping through in the tossing wind, but enough remain to whisper, when everything else is still.

ACKNOWLEDGMENTS

WITH THANKS TO my agent Dorian Karchmar, my editor Jack Macrae, and assistant editor Supurna Banerjee; it's all been a pleasure. Everyone else—if you think your name should be here, I'm sure you're right.

ABOUT THE AUTHOR

MARY SWAN is the winner of the 2001 O. Henry Award for short fiction and is the author of the collection *The Deep and Other Stories* published by Random House. Her work has appeared in several Canadian literary magazines, including the *Malahat Review* and *Best Canadian Stories,* as well as American publications such as *Harper's.* She lives with her husband and daughter near Toronto.

Q&A with Mary Swan

1. Where did you get the idea for this story? What about the time period and subject matter appealed to you? Did you set out to write a novel?

The first spark came from something I happened upon several years ago—an account in a publication of a local historical society, of a man who had been tried and executed in the late nineteenth century for killing his family. I can't really explain why that story caught me, but I did know immediately that I would do something with it. Some time later, I started to write a short story about a young boy who had witnessed this execution, and for some reason he watched it from a tree overlooking the jail yard. But of course this boy had a home, and a family and friends, and I began to see that there were many other people connected to the story, and many different ways to tell it.

2. Naomi suffers the loss of her first three children to diphtheria, and thereafter moves from England to Canada, where her husband's troubles drive their small family from town to town. Mrs. Robinson, the doctor's wife, likewise finds herself living a life she would not choose for herself. What did you hope to convey about the condition of women, either in general or in this particular situation?

When writing about the past, it's important for me to really have a sense of what it was like to experience the world as an individual living in a particular time, and that means recognizing limitations as well as the thoughts and feelings and situations that are constant. Historically, women's lives have been particularly restricted by their biology, economic dependence, and lack of political power. I don't write to convey a message, but I did have that fact very much in mind when thinking about and creating the female characters in *The Boys in the Trees*.

3. The narration of the story switches from character to character to great effect; however, one significant perspective is missing. Did you deliberately avoid including a section from the point of view of the adult William Heath?

Yes, I knew from the beginning that I wouldn't have a section from Heath's point of view, just as I knew that I wouldn't deal any more directly than I have done with the murders themselves. To have done either of those things would have made it a different kind of book. I suppose that I am most interested in the ripples caused by events, and the way so many things, especially human beings themselves, are ultimately unknowable.

4. At the end of the novel Eaton looks back on the town's reaction to the murders, which linger in his memory. Did you always plan for the novel to span multiple generations?

That wasn't part of my plan, but then again I didn't have much of a plan when I began to write the book, only an idea of a number of things and characters that I wanted to explore. At a certain point, however, I began to feel a need to somehow bring things forward, and to give an idea of what might have happened to some of the characters, without using a neat, summative epilogue. In thinking about it now, I suppose that I was also not ready to let them go, if that makes any sense. I particularly didn't want to leave Eaton stuck in that tree, without the suggestion that his life was all right, in the end, when it easily might not have been. Not exactly a happy ending, but as close as I'm likely to come to one.

5. What resonance, if any, does this story have with your own personal experience? Are the themes of family and memory ones that you have explored in your other works?

When I began thinking about this story, the idea of family was central to what I wanted to explore. I thought a lot about happy families and miserable ones, about lost families and damaged families, and about how much of our sense of belonging in the world is bound up in that relationship, in one way or another. The importance of memory ties into that, of course, and it does seem to work its way into almost everything that I write.

6. Your writing in this novel is very suggestive, details and their meaning rising slowly to the surface as the story progresses. Was this style particular to *The Boys in the Trees*?

I don't think it's particular to *The Boys in the Trees;* more likely a function of the way my mind works. Things usually take a very long time to gel for me, and I can walk around for months half-thinking about something I want to be writing, my pockets filling up with scraps of paper where I've scribbled phrases or ideas as they bubble up. It wouldn't be true to say that I don't have any kind of plan, or any idea about the direction I want for a story or the connections I want to make. But those things really only happen through the process, when I actually start writing the story.

7. You've captured the interior lives of young and old, male and female, with deft assurance. Did you find any section or character particularly difficult to write?

I started a number of versions of the "Forgiveness" section before I worked out one I was content with, and I think that a lot of the difficulty had to do with the character of Sarah, whose intensity and joylessness are quite alien to me. I was trying to find a way to communicate some kind of sympathy or understanding for a character who is not, to me at least, particularly likeable. Also, as I mentioned earlier, I began by trying to write what is now the last section, "Eaton—1889," but didn't get very far. I came back to it a number of times while I was working on the rest of the book, but it wasn't until I thought of using dime novels that I was able to actually write it from beginning to end.